Spells for Victory
and Courage

SPELLS FOR VICTORY AND COURAGE

Stories

by

DANA FITZ GALE

BRIGHT
HORSE
BOOKS

Printed in the United States of America

Brighthorse Books
13202 N River Drive
Omaha, NE 68112
brighthorsebooks.com

ISBN: 978-1-944467-01-2

Cover Art © Christophe Boisson

TABLE OF CONTENTS

For my family,
with love and gratitude

Spells for Victory
and Courage

Schooling

Arithmetic:

Arithmetic is easy. Forty bucks, placed on the dapple gray (Win, Place or Show) equals a cool three-hundred—glory be. Dumont, your paraplegic father, peels two twenties off the top and hands the rest to you, for safekeeping. Off he wheels to buy a celebration liter of Crown Royal. You, meanwhile, will do some shopping at the IGA adjacent to the racetrack parking lot. Dumont subsists on Fritos and beef jerky, but lately you've developed a mild interest in nutrition, so you toss a box of whole-wheat crackers in the cart, on top of boxed potatoes, powdered eggs, and tunafish. Ignore the cashier when she asks how old you are and why you aren't in school, this time of day.

Back at the lot, inside the Winnebago you call home, remember to tuck several bills into the zippered pencil case beneath your bunk. (Don't worry, you can tell Dumont those groceries cost more than they really did. He never asks to see receipts). The remainder will be wagered on that blaze-faced chestnut in the three-fifteen, a horse called Lightning Finish, who will—sadly—prove unworthy of that name.

History:

A subject best ignored. You know full well it's better not to aggravate Dumont with questions on the subject of your mother, including who she was (she was sixteen when you were born, that's all you know) and where she went, or why she left before you had a chance to get acquainted. It is especially prudent to avoid this subject when Dumont's been drinking—which is all the time.

Geography:

Dumont, possessing better social skills than most ex-jockeys, has become quite good at handling snoops and busybodies. He tells strangers, when they ask, that you and he are visiting from Murfreesboro, Tennessee. The two of you are in whatever town you're in to visit his wife's mother. You happen to be at the track because, like many girls your age, you have a thing for horses. So the story goes.

The truth is, though you've lived at eighteen racetracks, in a dozen states, you've never even been to Tennessee—a place where gambling is illegal. Dumont just likes the way that word sounds, "Murfreesboro," and besides, he figures, nobody's from there.

Home Economics:

When supplies get low, mix extra water in the dehydrated milk. A little duct tape helps to keep the damp out of your boots. Make sure to check beneath the grandstands daily—you'd be amazed at how much spare change falls from race fans' pockets. Dumpster diving is undignified, unsanitary, best reserved for true emergencies like month-long losing streaks, or times when no one wants to pay a girl for odd jobs, pulling manes and cleaning stalls. Whatever happens, try your utmost not to touch the secret savings in your pencil case.

Physics:

Fourteen hundred pounds of horseflesh coming round the curve, colliding with the rail at thirty miles an hour will catapult a small-boned man at least ten yards, into the path of a whole field of thoroughbreds which, moving on the same path at a roughly equal speed, deliver the force needed to obliterate a jockey's spine between the second and third lumbar vertebrae.

A horse would never be allowed to suffer so.

Health:

If your father were a thoroughbred, he would be dead, and you—who've had the sore luck to be born a filly in this no-frills world—had better not forget to watch your back. Stick to the lighted portions of the stableyard, befriend the oldest groom at every track, in hopes that you'll remind him of his grandchild, back in Guadalupe, and—if all else fails—recall Dumont's advice: a metal hoof-pick makes the perfect implement for gouging eyes.

Chemistry:

Dumont's prescription pain pills, mixed with gin, can sometimes make him mean as snakes. It isn't that he wouldn't hit you, if he could, but you are quicker, nimbler, having two good legs. Sometimes, when he believes you've been neglecting him, because you've been out scrounging all day long to keep your bellies full, Dumont will howl that you are all the same, you females, treacherous and cruel. If you laugh (he is a spectacle, this tiny, raging, helpless man) he'll start in on his threats, the same ones you've been hearing all your life. He'll say, for instance, that he'll hunt you down and beat you senseless with a nickel-plated stud chain if you ever try to leave him like she did, ungrateful slut. When he starts talking this way, tip his wheelchair forward till he slides out. It won't be hard—he's such a featherweight. Be sure to clear the area of any objects he might throw before you leave him stranded on the floor, to curse and flail until his eyes roll back. Then place a folded sheepskin saddle pad beneath his snoring head and gently— very gently—roll his body to one side. You don't want him to choke.

Music:

First, the trot: a pair of eighth notes, alternating. The canter has a three-fourths tempo, like a waltz. The gallop is a symphony in four-four time, and is the soundtrack of your father's dreams. You know this from the way his whip hand lifts and falls when he's asleep, and from the rhythmic spasms of his shoulder muscles.

Art:

A horse's breath is silver in the cold hours after dawn. Dumont and you are stationed in your customary place along the rail, between the first and second furlong markers. It doesn't matter that you watch the morning workouts every day, they still affect you. Every time a group of horses thunders by, you hold your breath. Your father grips the edges of his wheelchair, pushes up and forward, arms taut, neck out, like he's trying to fly. At times like this, you wonder if your secret plan requires courage, or mere heartlessness.

Biology:

You learn this soon enough. Your teacher is a stable-hand named Luke, your classroom is an empty stall, a week before your sixteenth birthday. You'll find the subject disappointingly simplistic, at the start, but will be quick to see how it might help to further your ambitions.

Philosophy:

Sometimes, hung-over, Dumont turns all misty-eyed and metaphorical. He rolls past the rows of horses in their stalls, comparing them to inmates in a jail. He reaches up to stroke the muzzle of some wild-eyed two-year-old who wears a sharp-edged metal yoke around his wind-pipe. He says he hates those goddamn cribbing collars. He tells you only captive horses have bad habits. All race-horses are cribbers, kickers, weavers, says Dumont. Or biters. Who can blame them? Dumont shakes his head and mutters in a voice almost too low to hear, that all caged things possess the memory of freedom.

English:

English hurts. The past tense of the verb *to leave* is *left*, as in she left while he was sleeping, having slipped two ground-up pain pills in his drink. The antonym of *love* is *loss*. *Betrayal* is a synonym for *daughter*.

Arithmetic:

It all comes back to this. Combine that fourteen hun-dred in your pencil case with the wad of C-notes Du-mont hands you for safekeeping, after he finally hits the daily double. Add, subtract. The sum is equal to a brand new start in life.

However things turn out, don't blame your math. Hold your equations firmly in your head so you won't falter as you tiptoe past his bunk, won't stop to watch his whip hand rise and hover.

Think about the money. It'll last, so long as Luke's truck doesn't throw a rod in Escondido and he doesn't spend a bundle on his hitherto-concealed cocaine ad-diction. These things, or course, may never happen, just as Luke may never leave you broke and stranded at some highway rest stop—in which case, you can keep believing that you have an eye for winners.

Either way, it doesn't change things. Doesn't change the fact that, years from now, after you've given up on searching and have sworn off racetracks altogether, you'll still be convinced you hear him, now and then. Not Luke, your father. You'll be walking down some street, your mind on other things, and all at once, you'll think you hear his slurred voice calling you. Always and everywhere, you'll hear him: cursing, spitting, aching to forgive.

Leah, Lamb

THE REVEREND SPAIN HAS asked her for a photograph
and—since Leah has no pictures of herself—she has to
ask her landlady to snap a Polaroid, when the landlady
stops by, collecting rent. She poses outside, next to her
screened porch, because the tigerlilies are in bloom and
Leah hopes the flowers will compensate for what she
lacks in terms of looks. The Reverend has assured her
that he doesn't care about such things, it is her purity of
soul that he admires, but Leah thinks a man like him,
who's done so much to help the children of the world,
deserves to look at something beautiful. Also, she wants
him to see what kind of house she lives in, and what
kind of town: hence, Main Street in the background
with the picture house, all boarded up, and hence the
bar with its apologetic sign: "Trail's End Saloon." Her
church is on the same block, but the whitewashed stee-
ple of Atonement Lutheran does not materialize in the
photograph. There's just the defunct theater and the
neon bar sign. She is glad. Leah doesn't want the Reverend Spain to pity her. She just wants him to understand why she can't send more cash than she does, every
month, to help with his important work in Africa.

She inscribes the photo with his first name. "Dell-
Mar, this is me." It seems like such audacity, calling
an ordained minister by his first name, especially one

she's never met in person. Yet he calls her Leah, always, in his letters. Lately, he's started writing "Leah, dearest" and, once, "Leah, lamb," which makes her feel all jittery, remembering. She hopes that he won't think she is forward, calling him "Dell-Mar." She's warned him that she is a rookie when it comes to love, that she, approaching fifty years of age, has never kissed a man besides her husband Arnold, and that, since Arnold's disappearance, many years ago, she has resigned herself to solitude—or had, until the Reverend Spain dropped into her life, lighting up her skies like Sputnik One, aflame.

She mails the photograph the next day, on her way to work. On Sundays, Leah worships at Atonement Lutheran, and most other mornings, she goes there to clean. She's worked here since she first arrived in town, at the beginning of the war, and every day for the past twenty years, she's thanked her savior for her job within His house. She likes the church on Sundays, all the pick-up trucks and Studebakers parked out front, the farmers in their Sabbath finery, the fancyhatted wives, but she likes it better when the congregation's gone. She loves the soft groans of the floorboards and the radiant-colored squares of light that pulse and quiver there, like living things. Sometimes—and this is something she has not told anyone, not even Reverend Spain—sometimes when she is rubbing lemon oil into the pews, she can detect a faint noise coming from the altar. She hears the sweetsad singing of a microscopic choir. She can't hear this on Sunday mornings, though. It only happens when she's all alone.

She's not alone this morning. Pastor Larson's in his office, working on a sermon. His door is open. She can see his crewcut head bent low over his typewriter and she tries not to distract him as she gets her mop and broom out of the closet, but he looks up, anyway. "Say, Leah. I liked those nifty thingamajigs you made for the craft bazaar," he says. "Those were just swell." Leah is fond of Pastor Larson, but it bothers her, the way he uses so much slang. His predecessor never talked that way.

"How did you think of using corncobs for the handles?" Pastor asks.

She shrugs. "When I was young, we just used what we had. We didn't throw things out, like nowadays."

"Oh. Well. They were nifty doodads, anyhow."

"People now throw everything away. Good clothing. Vacuum cleaners. Food. When there are people starving overseas."

He gazes at her with that worried face he sometimes gets.

"All those precious little children," she says. "Starving."

"Yes." He runs one hand over his bristly scalp, exhales, and goes back to his work.

She cleans the sanctuary first. She mounts the three steps to the pulpit, sweeps the sacred hexagonal space inside, then dusts the rails, applying extra pressure to the smoothdark fingershapes where Pastor Larson rests his hands on Sundays. She will not allow herself to wonder what it feels like to be standing there, in front of an entire congregation, sermonizing. She is not prone to foolish flights of fancy; vanity is not among her flaws. Though she has other flaws, of course. She is a sinner born; she's done bad things, the same as every human being. For instance, it is probably a sin that she delights in solitude, that she prefers the church without the congregation present. Why should she wish to hoard the Savior to herself? She decides to ask the Reverend Spain this question soon. Quite often, they discuss theology within their letters.

Assuming that there will be any further letters, once he's seen her photograph. He says he doesn't care about appearances, or not the temporal kind, at least. He's promised her that when they finally meet, he'll see her as she'll look on Judgment Day, all wreathed in glory, but she's sure he will be disappointed, nonetheless. She is not vain, yet nor is she abashed at how God made her, plain and capable, no curves except her spine, a bit curled over at the top. She is less hourglass than apostrophe, but not abashed. She just can't fathom how a man who looks like Reverend Spain (thick silver beard and hair swept straight back from his temples just like Charlton Heston's in *The Ten Commandments*, which was the first and only moving picture Leah saw before the picture house shut down) could fall in love with her.

THE PROPHET MOSES, PARTING the Red Sea. That's what she thought when she first saw the Reverend at the open-door revival meeting in the country. Dell-Mar (does she really dare to call him that?) had bowed his head to bless a child with a clubfoot and his sterling mane shone fiercemajestic and the whole crowd under that green army tent exhaled amen. Amen. She'd gone there because she had seen the posters and heard people talking in the supermarket—the Reverend had been holding meetings for a week in the next county over, not too far away, and Leah was curious. So on the night of the last meeting, she drove thirty miles in the old rusted-out jalopy she'd inherited from Arnold, and found the tent pitched in a cattle pasture, by the river. She was relieved not to see anyone she knew.

The meeting lasted more than three hours, until well past dark. She was interested in the healing, in the laying on of hands. She was curious because this was a thing that never happened in the Lutheran church and she noticed that the preacher was good-looking—very!—but she didn't feel the spirit move her, even when the crowd all stood and swayed, hands raised, or when the woman next to her began to speak in tongues and then fell, writhing, on the grass. In fact, she wished the woman would get up. Leah disapproves of histrionics, as a rule.

Nor did she feel the presence of the Holy Ghost when the Reverend started dunking people in the river— she'd watched baptisms aplenty at Atonement. But later, when the baptizing was over and the moon cast patterned shadows on the water and the Reverend started preaching in his silky baritone about the spread of intellectual agnosticism, which was incubated in the Eastern cities and then radiated out, like cancer, like bubonic plague, infecting young and old with feverish ideas, inclining them toward liquor, gambling, rock and roll, and creeping communism, marijuana, slothfulness, licentiousness of thought and deed—she stood up with the others, raised her palms. The Almighty needed help, the Reverend said, expunging all that was unwholesome in the land, and though Leah knew he couldn't see her in the back row, she still felt as if he were addressing her, alone.

"Are you okay?" It's Pastor Larson. She was not aware that he was in the sanctuary, never heard him coming in, and now she wonders how long he has been here, watching while she daydreams in his pulpit. She backs down the steps, all three at once, and starts to sweep, making the dust rise up into a swirling vortex of the kind that smothered crops when she was young. The pastor clears his throat. "I've been meaning to ask you something, Leah." He has that worried look again. "I was wondering if you would like to take some time off work."

She gapes. He's only been a pastor for a year, whereas his predecessor guided First Atonement for three decades. Does this young man have the arrogance to fire a twenty-year employee?

"I mean, a short vacation," he says. "Just a little break. You haven't taken a week off since I've known you." It's been longer than that. Longer than this freckled baby-pastor can imagine, but she only says, "I don't need a vacation. I enjoy my work."

"Don't you have relatives, somewhere, that you would like to visit?"

"No," she shakes her head. "No family. It's just me and Buster."

Pastor blinks.

"Buster's my cat. He's an orange tabby."

"Oh." He coughs. "Well, think about it, anyway. There must be someone you would like to visit, if you had the chance."

She flushes. There is someone, but he can't know that. Leah has not told anyone about her correspondence with the Reverend, which has lasted eight months now. It's not that she's embarrassed—there is nothing scandalous within those letters. She just knows no one would believe her, if she told. Not just because most Lutherans do not go to tent revival meetings, but also because Leah looks nothing like those ladies in the magazines, the ones who've obviously never swept the dirt floor of a sod house, never wrung a rooster's neck, not even once, never gathered dried-up cowchips to burn in the stove for winter heat. She knows she's an unlikely romance heroine and she is sure that Pastor Larson would be skeptical, especially if he knew about the money she's been sending, every month, to help the children in the Belgian Congo.

It isn't his fault that he wouldn't understand. It's just that Pastor, with his rosy cheeks, his pencilcalloused hands fresh from the seminary in Nebraska, has obviously never lacked for food. In her first letter to Dell-Mar, Leah explained how she had grown up motherless in Oklahoma, in a sod-roof dugout, where she'd often fried up lumps of flour and water to feed her father and herself because the flour was all they had, unless one of them shot a possum or a quail, and he responded that he'd known privation, too. He was an orphan, which was why he felt a special kinship with those orphans in the Congo. "You and I," he wrote, "are cut from the same cloth, dear Leah. We both know what it is to suffer and your suffering will not go overlooked when it comes time to separate the righteous from the damned." His words brought her more consolation than he could have guessed, though Leah fears it was a sin, the way she shoved the poor cat off her lap, reading those words, because her lap was suddenly too warm.

"A paid vacation, naturally," says Pastor Larson now. "Wouldn't you like to take a week off with full pay? Or even two?"

"Perhaps," says Leah. "I'd need some time to think about it." Then, as he leaves the sanctuary, she says, "Wait."

He turns around, expectant. "Yes?"

"Could I borrow your typewriter, after my work is done?"

"Again?"

"I'll pay you for the ribbon."

"No, no. That isn't what I meant. It's neat that you've been doing so much typing, Leah. Are you taking a correspondence course or something?"

"No." Leah does not return his smile. "Of course not. I just need to write a letter." If he asks, she will explain that she prefers to type because her penmanship is wretched, a result of never having gone to school. The school was too far from her home and anyway, her father needed help around the house. He taught her everything he could: to read the Bible, copy verses and to cipher numbers. Also, the way to load and fire a twenty-two and how to gut small game, which came in handy later, when their crops began to fail. He taught her well, but penmanship was not among her father's strengths. However, Pastor doesn't ask. He says, "Feel free to use the typewriter at any time, Leah. There's no need to ask."

Dear Reverend, Leah types, an hour later, after Pastor Larson has gone home and she has finished with her work. She isn't brave enough to call her beau by his first name today. *By the time you get this, you'll have seen my photograph. I mailed it this morning. I warned you that I wasn't much to look at. I guess you'll believe me now.* Leah bites her lip and keeps on typing with two fingers, flinching every time the carriage return richochets across the page. *I had to write again so soon because there's something that I need to tell you. I should have told you sooner but I wasn't sure how to explain it. Please forgive my—*. Leah stops to fix her error, changes "my" to "me", continues pecking at the keys until the letter is complete —a whole page and a half. She puts it straight into an envelope and seals it up. Writes "AIR MAIL ONLY" in block letters next to the address in Tennessee, which is where the Reverend makes his home when he's not on the road, holding revival meetings, or in the Congo, with the orphans there.

She intends to mail the letter on her way back home,

but then changes her mind. She doesn't want it to arrive before the photograph. The next day she has funeral committee and she's too busy prepping food for the Copenhaver funeral to even think about the Reverend. That's not true. She thinks about him plenty, while she's gouging eyes out of potatoes, chopping onions for the stroganoff, enough to feed a hundred Lutherans, give or take a few. And later, when she's in her nightgown, combing out her hair, she shuts her eyes and thinks about the laying on of hands. Maybe she won't send that letter, after all.

She does mail it, but not for three more days. She drops it in the mailbox on her way to Hobson's farm, for quilting circle. The Hobson place is less than five miles out of town. Noreen Hobson greets her at the door, with a baby on one shoulder and a toddler tugging at her skirt. Leah hands her hostess a small pair of crocheted socks. "Here. I made them green because I couldn't remember what it was, this time. Is it a boy?"

"A girl," Noreen says. Leah follows her into the living room, where a group of women are already seated near the quilt frame, basting. "We missed you last week," Noreen says. "Were you sick?"

"No. Busy." Busy reading up about the Belgian Congo at the library, if anybody asks. Of course, nobody does.

Noreen sets her baby in a playpen with some others, tries to pry the toddler from her leg. "You probably didn't notice," she says, "but we got ourselves a brand new member, since the last time you were here."

"Well, hello, Josie Larson." Leah turns to smile at

Pastor's wife. "I didn't realize you were a quilter."

"I'm not much of one." Josie fingers her pearl earrings, acting shy. She's younger than her husband, even. In her wool, pleated skirt and ankle socks, she looks like she belongs in high school, though she must be twenty-one or two, at least. "I'm not much good, to tell the truth. I'm not like you. But I did buy some gingham, to make squares."

Noreen, meanwhile, has extricated herself from the toddler, but no sooner has she managed this than another child appears from nowhere and starts pulling at her wrist. Leah doesn't think she's seen this child before, but then, it's hard to keep them straight. "Take heed, Josie," says Noreen, with a sigh. "See what your future holds?"

"Oh, I love children," Josie smiles.

"You say that now."

Josie holds up a piece of fabric, so that everyone can see. "What do you think? I ordered it from the Sears Roebuck catalog. I thought it might look pretty in a Sunburst pattern, maybe."

Amid a general murmur of appreciation, Leah says, "You purchased that brand new? How much?"

"Pay no attention, Josie." This is Noreen's cousin, Deb. "She thinks we're all supposed to use old rags to piece our tops."

"It was on sale," says Josie. "Fifteen percent off."

Leah moves over to the quilt frame. "You see that?" she taps the border of the quilt. "And over there, the squares inside the star? And there? Those all came from a bedsheet I got for a wedding gift. I used it for ten years and then I turned it and used it another ten before I tore it up for scraps."

"Leah," Noreen says, "maybe you could help me get the coffee?"

"Do you know what it means to turn a sheet?" says Leah to Josie, and the younger woman shakes her head.

"You use it until it wears thin in the middle," Leah says, "and then you slit a line straight down the center," similar to how one slits a possum, chin to tail, but Leah keeps this thought to herself. "You turn the outside edges in and make a new seam there, where the fabric's still intact. Your sheets will last you twice as long, that way."

"Of course, Leah's bedsheets don't see that much use," says Noreen, winking. "Most of us wear the sheets out quicker, if you catch my drift."

"For shame," says Deb. "You're making Josie blush."

"You young people buy everything brand new," says Leah, pretending not to hear the snickering. "Brand new. It's such a waste."

"Don't mind her, Josie," says Noreen. "Leah was raised in dustbowl country, don't forget. In a dugout house, no less."

"A dugout?" Josie says. "I've never heard of that. You mean . . . underground?"

Leah nods. "My father built it right into the hillside. Reinforced the door with stones so it would hold up when the milk-cow grazed over our heads. The doorway was an arch because an arch is stronger than a door with corners. My father said the ancients taught us that."

"The floor was dirt," says Deb.

"Of course. But I made braided rugs to cover it. And we pinned flour sacks to the walls. I had to take the sacks down once a week to shake the bugs out, but it's cozy in a sod house. Warm and snug. The dust blew right over our heads. We had it better than most people, in those days. The weather rolled right over us and kept on going. That's why a dome-roofed building lasts so long. Think of the Taj Mahal."

"The Taj Mahal."

"We didn't have it bad," says Leah. "Believe me, plenty others had it worse, back then. It's cozy in a sod house." True enough, until the grass dried up and blew away and then the milk cow dried up, too, which was possibly what caused Leah's spine to curl, the lack of calcium. And not too long after the passing of the cow, her father died, and then it seemed she had no choice except to marry Arnold, whom she met in town, who seemed like a good Christian man, at first.

The baby in the playpen starts to wail and Noreen checks her watch. "She's still got half an hour till feeding time," she says. "See what you got in store for you, sweet Josie?" Josie smiles, smoothing the folded gingham in her lap. The infant's cries get louder. "And Leah, count yourself among the fortunate. You don't have to put up with anybody but yourself."

"I'll second that," says Deb. "I'm sick and tired of Eric tracking mud across my rugs. How many times I've told that man to take his boots off at the back door, I can't say. And then his socks stink something fierce.

Worse than his shirts."

"You're lucky, Leah," Noreen picks her screaming baby up, at last. "I envy you." She says things like this all the time, but Leah knows she's not sincere. Noreen, with her wailing offspring and her pablumcrusted green formica tabletop, her new pink Westinghouse refrigerator and her matching stove, would never trade her life for Leah's. Nor would Deb, her husband's odors notwithstanding. Leah knows how people talk about her when she's not around. Poor Leah. Her husband up and disappeared when she was still a newlywed and now she's growing old with just a cat for company and not a penny to her name.

Leah doesn't care what people think and anyway, they've got a few things wrong. It's true, the memory of hunger haunts her; sometimes still, she starts to salivate when she spots a raccoon up a tree, or an unusually plump squirrel. She will remember hunger, always, and the snugness of her subterranean abode: the glow of cowchips burning and the smell of roots and clay and earthworms—but she rarely thinks of Arnold anymore. Her time with him was brief, the Lord be praised. And also, she is not as poor as people think. In fact, she has one hundred twenty thousand dollars in a rainy day fund. One hundred twenty thousand, unbeknownst to anyone except herself and—very soon—the Reverend Dell-Mar Spain.

She told him all about it in her letter, told him how the money was the only thing she ever got from Arnold, unless you counted his old car and her black eyes, her busted ribs. She found it in a cardboard box beneath the bed, a few weeks after Arnold disappeared for good. Back then, it was a little over fifty thousand, all in hundred dollar bills—a tidy sum, in 1938—but she invested it in Standard Oil shares and it multiplied, just like the fishes and the loaves. She still has no idea where the money came from. When he wasn't at home, smacking her around, her husband kept low company, she knew. She heard that he consorted with known criminals, with gamblers, thieves, loose women—he was rumored to have tried his hand at everything, except for honest work, which is why she hasn't spent a dime of what he left behind, and why she's kept the money secret for so long. She assumed that nobody as virtuous as Dell-Mar Spain would want to hear about her former husband's sin, but now, she told the Reverend in her letter, she has changed her mind. She's realized that something good might still be wrought from Arnold's legacy—it's not too late. His tainted fortune could bring sustenance to children in a faroff land, and wouldn't that be a fine aggravation to the devil?

"Leah," Noreen says. "Would you help me bring the coffee out? It's hard to do with just one hand."

"Here, let me hold the baby," Josie puts her arms out. "Please, Noreen."

A WEEK GOES BY without a letter from the man she loves. Of course, Leah didn't expect a speedy answer—it takes time for mail to travel, even air mail, and besides, more than half the time he isn't home in Tennessee but on the road, somewhere, spreading the Word. Sometimes he is in the Belgian Congo, and then she might hear nothing for a month or more. She knows this—she reminds herself of these things every day—yet by the third week she's convinced that she will never hear from him again. By now, he must have seen her photograph. He's probably appalled—if not by her appearance, then by what she told him in her letter, about Arnold's money. It's Leah's own fault, she knows, that she didn't try to find the rightful owners of that cash, her own poor judgment that she never called the sheriff and she won't blame the Reverend if he ends his correspondence with her now.

By the close of that month—twenty days without a letter from the Reverend—Leah fears she is about to lose her mind. She forgets to put her mop-bucket away at work, leaves it sitting out beside the altar, right where everyone can see it, Sunday morn. The next day she puts a chicken in a broasting pan and then neglects to turn the oven on so when she comes home, nine hours later, her dinner is still raw—and worse, it's spoiled, unsafe for Buster, even. Looking at the wasted chicken, Leah weeps. Weeps for her younger, hungry self and all the hungry people in the world. Weeps for the love she had for a short while and now has lost. At night, she twists and turns until the cat decides it's safer to sleep in the other room and the center seam of Leah's perfectly turned sheet begins to fray. Instead of mending it, or saving it for scraps, she throws it out. And then, when she has given up all hope, a letter comes.

It's in the box when she gets home from work. She doesn't read it right away. She forces herself to eat dinner first, then cleans the dishes, puts her nightgown on, though it is only half past six, not even dark. She turns the lights down, all except the lamp next to her bed, and climbs beneath her quilt to read the letter. She reads all the Reverend's letters in her bed. She reads this one three times, from start to finish, her lips moving without sound. Buster purrs and rubs against her arm, to no avail. She doesn't even notice he is there.

She has the next two days off work—a blessing, since there's so much to be done. She pulls all the remaining carrots in her garden, and then cleans her house from top to bottom, washes all the walls and windows, scrubs the shelves inside her kitchen cupboards. Sunday night, after she gets home from Copenhaver funeral, she stays awake in bed till after midnight, reading each one of the Reverend's letters in sequential order, several times. Not the Reverend, not the Reverend —Dell-Mar. She might as well get used to saying his name now.

The next day, she calls in sick to work for the first time in twenty years and drives out to the Hobsons's in the rain. Noreen greets her in curlers and a polka-dotted housedress. "Shh. Quiet. I just put Baby down to sleep."

Leah skirts past her to the kitchen, without waiting for an invitation. Her shoes are muddy and the cardboard box she's carrying is dripping wet.

"Making some jam?" Leah glances at the large pot on the stove.

"Boiling diapers," says Noreen. "What's in the box?"

"Diapers. Oh. I wondered what I smelt." Leah sets the box down on the kitchen table and Buster, inside, gives a plaintive mew.

"Leah, you brought your cat?"

"His name is Buster."

"You don't say. Why is he on my kitchen table?"

Leah opens up the box and lifts the cat out, sets him on the floor. A child appears from somewhere, tries to grab the cat, who darts beneath the sink. "I'm leaving town," says Leah. "Very soon. I figured a big farm like this could use a mouser."

"Leaving? Why? Oh, Charlie, leave that cat alone. He'll scratch you. Mind my words." To Leah: "Where're you going? For how long?"

"I'm going for good," says Leah. "I told my landlady already."

Noreen frowns. "You're not going back to Oklahoma? I thought you had no family left down there."

"I have no family anywhere."

The little boy screams and begins to cry. "Well, Charlie, what'd I tell you?"

Says Noreen. "It serves you right for pestering that cat." She shoos Charlie from the kitchen, fills a saucer up with milk.

"Buster likes his milk warmed up," Leah informs her, but Noreen puts the saucer down the way it is.

"You still haven't told me where you're going."

"Africa."

"I beg your pardon?"

"Africa. The Belgian Congo. They've got all these starving children over there."

"Ah," Noreen nods slowly. "Ah, you're doing volunteer work, then. You signed on with the Lutheran Women's Missionary League."

"Not exactly."

"Then you're going on your own?" Noreen smirks, as though she's made a clever joke. "You're giving me your cat so you can skip off to the Ivory Coast, all by yourself?"

"The Belgian Congo," Leah corrects her. "Not alone. I'm getting married."

There. She's said it, and now Noreen's smile is gone, replaced by an expression better, even, than the various expressions Leah has pictured in her head, since she decided to bring Buster here. Noreen's face, at this moment, is enough: sufficient compensation for the years of charitable smiles, the sideways glances and the under-the-breath jibes, the spinster jokes. Noreen pulls out a chrome and vinyl chair and sits, not bothering to cross her legs. For the first time since Leah has known her, Noreen does not have anything to say.

Leah fills the lapse in conversation with a few details about her fiancé. She tells Noreen about the Reverend's work in Africa, and that he's been her pen-pal for some time, but she does not disclose the circumstances of their meeting. Nor does she tell her friend about the money. "I appreciate you taking Buster off my hands," says Leah. "I know he'll like it, living on a farm, and I need to get my one-way Greyhound ticket, right away."

"You're going to Africa," says Noreen, "on the bus?" Her voice is dull, as if nothing she hears can possibly surprise her anymore.

"Well, no. I'm going to Chicago and St. Louis and then on down to Miami. I'll change buses twice. Miami's where we'll catch the boat." After the wedding, Leah assumes, although Dell-Mar was vague about the details, in his letter. "I'll take the bus because my car's so old and I'm afraid to drive on that new superhighway." Leah pauses, but Noreen says nothing. She is staring into space. "Besides," adds Leah, "I've been waiting for a chance to ride on one of those new Scenicruiser coaches. Have you seen the advertisements? 'Every mile a magnificent mile . . . every highway a strip of velvet.' They've got a lavatory, even. With an actual flush toilet."

Another pause, then Noreen speaks, her voice still strange and flat. "They have diseases over there in Africa. They've still got polio, I've heard."

"I've been vaccinated," Leah says. She pushes up the left sleeve of her dress to show Noreen the scar, as round and shiny as a silver dollar.

WITH BUSTER TAKEN CARE of, Leah finds it easy to make preparations for the trip. She doesn't own much. There's not much to pack. The only hold-up is her passport. She had not expected it would take so long to get one: several weeks! At least this gives her extra time to harvest what is still left in her garden, finish up her canning. When her passport finally arrives, she writes a note to Pastor, tells him that the rumors are correct—

she's leaving town. She wishes him and Josie all the best and hopes the church will find another cleaning lady soon. It would be courteous to tell him this in person, but she can't. Pastor Larson would be worried—he would ask all sorts of questions and she doesn't have the time for that right now.

She cleans the church the next day, same as always, leaves her note on Pastor's desk. Then she goes home and cleans her house for the last time, feeling no sadness for the rooms she's occupied so long. These stucco walls have sheltered her, yet they have never once embraced her like her childhood walls of dirt. Still, this is better than the house she shared with Arnold, certainly.

For supper, Leah eats a slice of bread with some pork gravy, using up the last remaining items in her fridge. She turns the lights off, loads her suitcase into her old car, atop the contents of her cellar: six boxes full of canned goods that cannot be left to go to waste. The furniture will stay behind, for the next tenant.

The bus depot is in the city, sixty miles away. It's nearly sundown when she gets there, since her car is slow and backfires constantly. The depot parking lot is almost full, but she finds a spot next to a bench, on which a homeless man lies sleeping. She knows this man, or knows his type. He looks just like the men who rode the rails, when she was young. She'd thought the hobos were all gone now, vanished with the war, yet here's one, grizzled, urinesmelling, wearing hobnail boots, all full of holes. His skin and clothes are the same hue, which is no color Leah can name, unless dust is a color. Yes, that's it—this man is dust, an apparition sent from 1936.

"Excuse me." Leah stands beside the bench. "Sir? Sir?" She touches the man's shoulder, which feels solid and unghostlike. He wakes up. "Here," she dangles her car keys before his eyes, and shakes them. "Here. Would you like a car?"

The man sits up. His face is angry. No doubt, he believes this is a prank. "No, really, you can have it," says Leah. "It's yours to keep. I can't take it with me, where I'm going. I don't know if they even have cars there."

The man looks worried now, as if he thinks she's talking about heaven. Still, he takes the keys. "Enjoy," says Leah. "If nothing else, it's a nice, warm place to sleep. And you'll find foodstuffs in the back. Non-perishables, mostly. Put some meat back on your ribs."

She joins the line of people on the platform. "Is this your only piece of luggage, Ma'am?" the driver asks. Leah nods, then watches as he flings her Samsonite into the cavedark cargo hold, down in the belly of the bus. She's not concerned; there's nothing valuable inside that case. The things that matter are inside her purse, strapped to her shoulder. All the money's there –the whole one hundred twenty grand, in travelers's checks. She was tempted to dip into it to buy herself a new dress for the trip, just something simple off the Penney's clearance rack, but she refrained. That money's for the orphans, every cent, and it's all there and accounted for inside her purse, just like her wallet and her reading glasses and her gout pills, her new passport and her pocket Bible (King James Version) and her gun. The gun belonged to Arnold, once—where else would Leah get a pistol?—and she's bringing it along for safety's sake, although it hasn't fired a shot in twenty years. She is a woman traveling alone, and there are some, in this swiftsinking world, who might attempt to take advantage of that fact.

She boards the bus, finds her assigned seat on the upper deck, beside a window. The turquoise seatcover is every bit as plush as she'd expected, from the advertisements, but she is dismayed to find that nearly all the passengers are smoking. Worse, the man across the aisle from her is swigging from a metal flask. Leah wonders if she ought to notify the driver. She hates the smell of whiskey—it brings back too many memories—so she unfolds a handkerchief and presses it over her nose and mouth.

Through her window, she can see the homeless man, still sitting on the hood of his new car. He's found a jar of Leah's pickled beets and his triumphant face makes Leah smile. It brings her joy to help the needy, always has. Dell-Mar says a sinful deed is like a tablespoon of dirt stirred into a clean glass of water—over time, the particles will settle and the water will look clear again, but the filth will be there always, bottomlurking, poised to re-contaminate the pure. He may be right, but Leah has no regrets.

She unsnaps her purse and counts the traveler's checks, again. All there. She has decided something, sitting on the bus. Dell-Mar must marry her immediately after she arrives in Florida. She will insist on this, since it might hurt his reputation to be seen consorting with a single woman like herself. Another thing, she won't give him the money, once they're wed. No, she is going to wait until they get to Africa, then give it to the orphans, place it right into their tiny hands. She will divide it up among them equally and give each child a share, in secret, telling them to hide it, guard it with their lives, use it for a college education or as a shield from future troubles, since you never know what hardships lie in store. You never know.

Outside, the hobo is still wolfing down the beets. Lucky for him, there are plenty more inside the car, enough to last him half the winter, probably. Leah takes pride in her pickled beets. Even Arnold said he liked them, which was probably the only kind thing Arnold ever said.

It isn't true that no one knows what happened to bad Arnold. No one knows except for Leah. Leah knows. She didn't want to but she had no choice and in the end, it wasn't all that hard—easier, by far, than killing some poor possum who had never done a thing to her. She knows she is forgiven, knows the Lord needs help—as Dell-Mar says—expunging evil from the land. And anyway, now she is off to save some orphans, and what better penance for a near-forgotten deed?

The Scenicruiser sputters, roars, and a blue shimmer of exhaust clouds Leah's view. She snaps her purse shut, holds the handkerchief a little closer to her face. Yonder, beyond the silhouettes of smokestacks, night is coming fast. The violet sky glows bright as kingdom come, while in the parking lot below, her hobo grins, his teeth stained iridescent red. Leah laughs into her handkerchief and waves at him. She will admit, she makes good pickled beets.

Jester

The most important part of Caleb's job is making sure the customers are angry, which comes naturally to him. He's always had a big mouth and a gift for pissing people off, his teachers, social workers and old Stobbs, the principal who kicked him out of tenth grade, just last year. And then there's Pop. When Caleb lived at home, his younger sisters used to beg him to be quiet when Pop came home after a hard day helping to unload dead horses at the rendering facility. But Caleb figured he was going to get it either way, he might as well give the old man some reason for his rage. And besides, Caleb's rudeness helped deflect attention from his mom. He'd take a dose of Pop's attention any time if it gave her a break.

But all that is behind him now. He's perched above a dunk-tank at a county fair in Idaho—or maybe it's Montana, he's not sure—a spotlight burning through the thick white greasepaint on his face, reflecting rainbows off his spangled hat. He wears a diamond-patterned jester's costume and has a microphone wired to a pole beside his head. His new friend Rocky's on the ground, enticing passersby. "This way, folks. Step right up. Two bones to drown the jester," Rocky says. "Two bucks a ball."

"Make sure you talk to that guy there," says Caleb, through his mike. "Him, there, in the big cowboy hat.

That gentleman looks like he needs some balls." The punch-line crackles through a hundred-watt P.A., but the cowboy doesn't even break his stride.

Nearby, two teenage girls are cracking up. Caleb thinks they look a little younger than himself. Fifteen or sixteen, max. One girl is taller than the other, with a sprinkling of pimples on her cheeks. "Did I say something funny, Pizzaface?" asks Caleb, and the tall girl puts her hands over her abdomen, like she's been shot. "Hey Pizzaface, what did you eat for breakfast, Ugly-Os?" She hurries off into the crowd.

He wishes that his former principal could see him now. Old Stobbs once told him, "Acting like a jackass isn't going to get you anywhere in life. Unless your aspiration is to be a circus clown." Well, look who's laughing now, huh, Mr. Stobbs? Caleb has always longed to see the world and now, at the tender age of seventeen, his dreams are coming true. He doesn't travel with a circus, but with a carnival called "Midway, U.S.A." In the past year, he's probably visited more states than that old fogey Stobbs will ever see.

A large man and a larger woman pass the dunk-tank, holding hands. "Hey Sir, nice pants," says Caleb. "Tell me, is that your belt holding them up, or the equator?" The man stops and looks around. The woman points at Caleb—big mistake. "Nice dress, Ma'am. By the way, the Ringling Brothers called. They're wondering what happened to their Big Top. Yuk, yuk, yuk!" The woman puts her hands over her face and the man turns towards Caleb. His expression is a mixture of bewilderment and loathing.

When the man takes out his billfold, Caleb smirks. Hook, line, and sinker. Bingo. Gotcha. Fat man's gonna sing.

Sometimes he feels a little sorry for the customers. Sometimes, he knows, he goes a little bit too far. Still, Caleb's only trying to do his job, and do it better than his predecessor, Rocky.

Rocky was the dunk-tank jester, up until they caught him selling weed behind the Tilt-a-Whirl. Then he got demoted to the ground crew—no big loss to Midway, U.S.A. Rocky never took much pride in jesting. He would doze off in his seat, waking, every now and then, to toss lethargic insults at the air. But Caleb's different. Caleb needs this job. He stays up late, inside the tractor trailer where he bunks with seven other men, reading old joke-books, whispering one-liners to himself. The secret is to make the insults personal, unique. You have to hurt the people where it counts so they'll spend every cent to take you down.

He twists and stretches. Rocky's right—after a few hours in this seat, your ass goes numb. At least it's not too warm here, in whatever state this is. Not like in Arkansas, last week, where his iron seat got hot enough to fry a steak and he had to cannonball into the tank to get relief because the hicks down there all threw like girls.

A boy, about twelve, with a shriveled leg, limps up and stops beneath the "Dunk the Jester" sign. "Well, don't just stand there, Slugger," Caleb tells him. "Buy a ball." The kid turns and hobbles off and Caleb shouts, "Hey, where you going, Gimpy? Are you chicken? Bwok, bwok, bwok!"

Caleb is not oblivious to irony. He's been called a gimp, and worse, himself, which is why he keeps his hand concealed beneath his nylon glove. But if these fairgoers won't hide their flaws, well, then they're asking for it, plain and simple. Anyway, they love it. Look, the line to dunk the jester is much longer than the Magic Carpet line. It's longer than the line to shoot at rubber duckies—longer, even, than the line to hurl blue ping-pong balls at plastic cups in hopes of winning a live goldfish in a bag. The Goldfish Game is genius. Caleb wishes he had thought of it himself. Five bucks, five throws and—every now and then—some lucky moron wins a ten cent feeder fish. Whoopee.

Private First-Class Trevor JAMES Beauchamps—called T.J. by civilian friends and family—is at the fair with his two kids: Sawyer, age seven, and Paige, who's just turned six. He's having a good time, or thinks he is. He isn't big on noise or crowds, but he remembers when he used to like these things and remembering counts for something, or it should. He got a fifteen percent discount at the gate for showing his I.D. Fifteen percent—not much having lived through Iraq and Afghanistan, and he wondered why he had to show his card when his T-shirt says Enduring Freedom on the front and lists his rank and regiment and squadron on the back. Still, the cashier had been nice enough. She'd thanked him for his service and gave stickers to the kids. She said, "I bet your mom is glad to have your dad home, safe and sound," and Paige—God bless her honest heart—informed her: "Daddy doesn't live at our house anymore."

They've only been here for a couple hours and the kids have been on nearly every ride their father will allow. Sawyer wants to try the Zephyr and he's tall enough, if he stands on his toes, but T.J. will not hear of it. "I don't trust the guys who put those things together," T.J. says.

Sawyer doesn't press the issue. He's always been such a good-natured kid. He acts as though he doesn't mind the Dizzy Dragons and the Kiddie Copters and the Squirt-sized Submarines, though T.J. knows his son is disappointed, not just about the Zephyr but about the corn-dogs, too. When they first arrived, the kids request-ed corn-dogs and some cotton candy. T.J. told them he'd brought sandwiches along. Maybe Shelley lets the kids fill up on junk food, nowadays. He won't.

Sawyer's interested in the Whirling Teacups but his sister says they'll make her puke, so they agree to try the Duckpond Game instead. T.J. shows his daughter how to hold her plastic rifle. "Keep it steady. Like this. Good. Now squeeze the trigger. That's the way."

There are things that happened overseas that T.J. can't remember now. Or he remembers, but it seems as if they happened to some other person or an actor in a movie, nobody he knows. His first deployment was the worst. There were days when all that kept him go-ing was the photo he kept in his wallet: Shelley and the kids posing with Santa, at the mall. One day, when he'd been gazing too long at the photograph, he put his foot through a glass door, got fifteen stitches and a referral for a mental health exam.

"Here"—he takes Paige's rifle—"let me try." He sights along the barrel at the bobbing head of the first duck. One down. He's still a good shot, never mind the tremors, a side effect of all these pills they've got him on. Three more. The ducks are coming faster now, just like the alien warships in that video game he liked to play, after Iraq. When he first came home, his kids behaved as if they didn't know him. Paige cried when he tried to pick her up.

Five ducks. His kids had gotten used to him, in time, but Shelley wanted him to go to counseling with her. She was the one who'd changed, not him. She fixed the broken screen door, mowed the lawn. She didn't seem to need him anymore. And she kept asking him why he was angry, when he wasn't. How could he be mad? Thanks to the pills, he mostly doesn't feel anything at all.

"Daddy," says Paige. "Can I have my gun back, now?"

"Hang on, sweetheart," he says. "I'm almost done."

After the duckpond, T.J. buys a pair of giant Sno-Cones at the FFA concession, paying no attention to the black flies buzzing all around the booth. Sure, he's overcompensating for the corndogs, but so what? He wants his kids to say good things about him, later, to their mom.

Then it's back across the midway, looking for the pony ride. The kids are slurping on their Sno-Cones; T.J.'s trying to stop thinking about toxic additives, carcinogenic dyes. He's having fun, he tells himself, yet he still jumps when he feels someone touch his arm. It's a civilian, just some guy wearing a black mesh shirt, which sags and billows on his bony frame. "Yo, Mister, wanna buy a ball?" the stranger leers. He has a barbed wire tattoo on his neck and the worst fingernails T.J. has ever seen. "Two clams to dunk the jester. Come on, man."

T.J. shakes him off and guides his children to the left, out of the stranger's reach. The guy has left a grimy handprint on his elbow. Jesus Christ. Why do these carnies always look as if they've never heard of soap?

A voice rings out. "Oh, Blondie, hey. Yoo-hoo! Hey, Wal-mart called. They need you, Blondie. They're fresh out of stupid."

Nearby, a woman stops and lifts one hand to her straw-colored hair. She turns and squints, and T.J. shades his eyes to see what she can see. Some kind of clown, he thinks, although it's hard to tell with that spotlight overhead and the sky darkening, behind.

"Hey, didja hear about the blonde who got run over by a parked car? Bada bing!"

Yep, it's a clown, all right. A strange one, with a moth-pale face and smeary, charcoal eyes. The clown leans to one side to spit and T.J. sees the guy is wearing jewelry as well as makeup: earrings and eyebrow studs and something silver glinting from his lip.

"Hey, soldier."

"Dad," says Paige. "That clown's talking to you."

"Hey Sarge, nice haircut. Wal-mart needs you, too. They're out of Brillo pads, I hear."

Paige giggles. T.J. nods, to show his kids he's a good

sport, but the clown, it seems, is not through with him yet. "Hey Sarge, I been wondering, how come they train you guys to walk like that? Like you got something up your a—ah-choo! Excuse me!"

"Dad," Sawyer whispers. "That guy's really rude."

"I know," says T.J.. "Keep on moving. Just ignore the clown."

CALEB WATCHES AS THE soldier walks away. Maybe he should have listened to his friend. When Caleb started, Rocky told him, "Rule of thumb. Don't pick on anyone who looks like they could kick your ass. Especially dudes in camo gear or wearing any kind of military medal." When Caleb asked him who would wear a medal to a carnival, Rocky just shrugged. "Beats me. But if you see a dude like that, it's best to keep your cakehole shut, okay?"

Well, what does Rocky know? He couldn't cut it as a jester. Caleb taunts anyone and everyone and so far, nothing bad has happened. This last guy doesn't even seem to care. Caleb can see him now, kneeling to tie his daughter's shoe outside the pony ride corral. The children's mouths are a bright, Sno-Cone blue, and the little girl has blue stains on her dress. The boy is carrying a Ziploc bag—aha, a lucky goldfish winner. The girl is holding a stuffed panda bear. You have to kill a lot of rubber ducks to win that panda, Caleb knows. In the whole year he's been with the carnival, he has not seen anybody win one of those bears before.

Another customer steps forward, takes her place

inside the chalk ring on the ground. Caleb knows her
—it's the girl that he dubbed "Pizzaface," although her
skin is not that bad, in truth. She throws a ball and
misses, then another. Caleb rattles off a few one-liners,
but his mind's not on his work. He's still watching the
soldier at the pony-ride corral.

The pony ride. When Caleb looks at ponies, he can
smell his father's clothes as vividly as if Pop hovered
there above the dunk-tank water. It was never just his
work clothes, either—all Pop's garments bore the faint
aroma of horse carcass, not excluding the brown suit he
wore to church. No wonder no one liked to stand beside
their family at communion. Caleb hates ponies, with
their drooping tails and sad, defeated eyes. Poor things.
If Caleb owned the pony ride, he'd have a sign: You
Must Be This Fucked-Up To Ride This Ride.

The soldier's kids are being boosted into saddles. The
boy's mount is too small for him; his feet are almost
dragging on the ground. Caleb hates ponies, so he shifts
his gaze back to the soldier, who is standing by the gate,
holding the goldfish-bag, the panda bear. This soldier
doesn't fiddle with his phone, like other dads. He doesn't
even turn to watch the small procession going by: a rodeo queen in rhinestone-studded chaps, with several
princesses in tow. He just watches as his kids go round
and round, and he waves at them when they go by. The
kids wave back, like it's some kind of thrill for them to
see him standing there, each time. Ridiculous and corny,
that's for sure. And yet.

Caleb ducks left to avoid a softball, whizzing past

his ear. Poor Pizzaface still hasn't called it quits. He tips his head back, gazes up into the spotlight, trying to dredge up some half-pleasant recollection of his father. His retinas glow white-hot, sparking haloes in his vision and he's six years old, again. He's in the small back yard at Grandma's house. His father plucks a ripe tomato from a plant and takes a bite, then hands the bleeding fruit to him. "Here, you can finish this one, Sport, but do it quick. You got to eat these in the first five minutes, else they turn to crap."

Is that it?, Caleb wonders, staring up into the light. Is that the sweetest childhood memory he has? His eyes are stinging, now, but he won't blink. And then the hinges underneath his seat snap shut—old Pizzaface has made a lucky shot; well, how about that?—and he is falling down, down, down into the tepid water, skidding on his side across the velvet bottom of the tank.

A CHEER GOES UP, but T.J. doesn't turn around. He has no interest in what's going on back there. He needs to focus on his kids to keep them safe. Hyper-vigilance, that's what the new shrink calls it. Pompous fool. These doctors use all sorts of big words, but they still can't tell him what went wrong with Shelley. They can't explain the way he acted when she stood before him in her new dress, just a month before she took the kids and left. In that dress, she was like the noon sun at Fallujah, but when she asked him why he wouldn't look at her, he couldn't tell her that she radiated light. Instead, he told her he was tired, which was the truth. And when their son, who was supposed to be asleep, ran in and threw his arms around his mother, T.J. told her, "See? See why I keep my mouth shut? Look what happens when I try to talk to you."

The pony ride is over. Sawyer's hungry. "Still?" says T.J. "You just ate a giant Sno-cone."

"Still. Can we get some cotton candy? Please, Dad? Please?"

"Yeah, Mom lets us eat cotton candy," Paige says, twining a long strand of hair around her finger. "All the time."

"Well, Dad pays all your dental bills," says T.J. There he goes again, making himself sound angry, when he isn't. He probably should be, since it sounds like Shelley has found someone new. The kids have mentioned somebody named Paul. "I'll tell you what," says T.J. "Let's do one more ride and then I'll take you both to get a smoothie at the mall. It's getting cold. Let's just do the bumper cars once more. Okay?"

The kids look dubious, but they cooperate. They follow T.J. through a haze of colored lights, past an old woman selling helium balloons and past the dunk-tank, where the clown is still haranguing passersby. T.J. is thinking about Paul. He wonders what Paul looks like. He tries to picture his wife with another man; he tries to picture them in bed. He tries to muster something, rage or jealousy, but all he feels is a mild tingling in his gut.

"Look, Dad, the clown's all wet," says Sawyer, pointing. "Someone dunked him, finally."

"It serves him right," says Paige. "That guy's so mean."

Her father smiles. "Well, that's his job, sweetheart." What kind of job does this Paul have, he wonders. Can Paul shoot a dozen rubber duckies in a row?

"Hey, Soldier." It's the clown, again. "Hey Sarge, forgot to tell you. Your wife called." T.J. stops.

"Uh-huh. She called me up to say she left her toothbrush at my place. Yuk, yuk, yuk."

"Why's he talking about Mom?" says Paige. "She isn't here."

"Yo, Sarge, she left her nightie there, as well."

"Gross," says Sawyer. "I don't get it."

Paige says, "Dad, you're squishing all my fingers."

The clown takes hold of the long fabric cones on each side of his hat, and pulls them down around his face, like hound-dog ears. "Don't take it personally, Sarge. She didn't tell me she was married."

"Ow!" says Paige, and T.J. lets go of her hand.

EVERYBODY HAS A SECRET button, Caleb knows. Even the coolest customers will lose their shit if he can find that button and keep pushing. Stobbs had one. The soldier has one, too—he must, but Caleb hasn't found it yet. He tries another joke about the wife, a lewder one. Rocky looks up, his mouth as slack as ever but his bloodshot eyes betraying a mild hint of curiosity. The soldier, though, seems unaffected, even after Caleb changes tack and starts suggesting that he's gay. "Don't ask, don't tell, right, Sarge? Wink, wink."

"Whatsha matter with you, Bozo?" An old man approaches Caleb. He has a stubbled chin and looks like he's been drinking steadily for days. "Don't shoe shupport our troopsh?" he slurs.

"Yo, Gramps, make like a ballerina. Split," says Caleb. "Find yourself a jug of Listerine and hunker down."

The soldier turns away and Caleb finds, to his surprise, that he is glad. There's something about Sarge that makes him hope he's wrong about the button thing. Maybe the soldier doesn't have one, after all. Maybe some men are different from the rest.

T.J. IS STARTING TO breathe normally again. Why get bent out of shape about some clown? Then Sawyer sneezes and the clown says, "Bless you." Not unkindly. He is smiling. Then he adds, "Hey, that's a nifty goldfish, Sport. Did you win that yourself? How old are you?" When Sawyer doesn't answer, he says, "What's wrong, Sport? Cat got your tongue?"

Next thing he knows, the waxy, lukewarm layer that shelters T.J. from the outside world dissolves. It's nothing in the words themselves—cat got your tongue—it's more the cadence of them and the angle of the sun, the smell of fried food and the distant sound of freight cars coupling and the way the asshole clown is smiling, scratching his left hand.

WELL, LOOK WHO'S JOINED the dunk-the-jester line. Surprise, surprise. Caleb had given up on Sarge, yet here he is, which proves that Caleb is the greatest jester Midway U.S.A. has ever known. Even when he isn't trying, he gets his man.

The line of customers is getting shorter now. The sun is going down. Caleb tucks his hands beneath his armpits, wishing that his costume weren't so wet. He isn't used to places where it gets this cool in August.

Sometimes at night, when Caleb rolls along some highway in the eighteen-wheeler, he sees back yards full of weeds and trash, brick houses where the curtains flicker with blue television-light. Or he sees houses with no curtains. Once, he saw two people having sex on a bare mattress and he laughed out loud, while the men around him slept. Another time, he caught of glimpse of wallpaper inside a kitchen—old-fashioned, peeling, with a blue rose pattern—and it filled him with a longing he could not explain.

The next few customers are nincompoops, and Caleb tells them this while trying to scratch his left palm through his glove. His hand still itches, all these years after the so-called accident. It itches and it stings, along the raised seams of the grafted skin. But the hand, at least, distracts him from his clammy costume, from the smell of popcorn, wafting in the air. It's been at least six hours since he ate lunch, and snacks are not allowed while he's on shift.

A ball rolls down the gutter. Caleb pulls his ruffled collar up around his face. Goddamn this wind. Goddamn this place. It's cold.

Last month, the carnival stopped over for a brief stint at a county fair within a hundred miles of his hometown. He thought of calling up his mother, just to hear her voice, see if maybe she would come and have a cup of coffee with him in the 4H tent. Then he remembered Pop, imagined his voice answering the phone instead of hers, and Caleb knew he couldn't call home, then or ever.

"WHO'S UP?" SAYS ROCKY. "Who's up next?"

"I am," says T.J., and he takes his place inside the chalkdust ring.

His hands are relatively steady, at the moment. He can keep them that way if he thinks about his breathing, if he concentrates on just one thing. It does no good to think about the other stuff, like how he'd like his wife to know he didn't reenlist to spite her, as she claimed. He just ran out of options. He didn't remember how to be a husband or a father but he knew how to be a soldier, still. And he thought maybe if he went back over to the sandbox, maybe he'd find what he'd lost there. He was wrong.

"Gee whiz, you're looking kind of trembly, Sarge," the clown says. "Maybe you should put the cork back in the bo—"

A splash. Applause. His children, laughing. "That was awesome, Dad," says Sawyer. "That was cool," and T.J. feels a slow heat radiating from his core.

"Yeah," Paige says, hopping up and down. "Do that again. Please, Dad?"

"Well," T.J. checks his billfold. He still has some money left inside.

•

IT'S HARDER THAN IT looks to hit that bullseye, Caleb knows. One time, in Alabama, some guy dunked him two times in a row and another time, some Texas smartass got him three times out of four, but this soldier is the first to sink him five times running. Uh-oh. Make that six.

From underwater, Caleb can hear garbled shouts and cheers. He sees kaleidoscoping greens and yellows, sees his own limbs moving in slow-motion. Each time he hits the bottom of the tank, it takes him longer to stand up. It's warmer underneath the surface than above. But he has to climb back in that seat because a crowd is gathering out there. He has to show those idiots who's boss.

Now IT'S OFFICIAL. T.J.'s having fun. Strangers are coming up to him, trying to shake his hand or slap his back. He winds up for another pitch and—it's a good one. Listen to those cheers.

Inside his mind, he's dedicating every throw to something he has lost. One for his wife. One for his kids. One for his self-respect. He's been on disability for six months now. The army doesn't want him back, thanks to his shaking hands and the exaggerated things the doctors wrote in their reports.

This throw is for the things he didn't say when Shelley left. She came downstairs and told him she was packed; the kids were waiting in the car. She asked him if he hated her and he didn't even look away from the T.V. "I don't hate anyone." That was the only thing he said.

"Are you finished yet?" asks Paige, her shrill voice ruining his concentration, yet again. "I don't like this. Anyway, the clown is cold, Dad. Look, he's shivering."

"So what?" says Sawyer. "Serves him right. Dad's going to knock him down again, right, Dad?"

"No. Sorry. We're done. I'm all out of cash."

"Here," says a man wearing a denim vest. "Take this," he puts a crumpled ten in T.J.'s palm. "You can't quit now, man. You're the best thing at this fair."

ROCKY, THAT TRAITOR, NEVER warned him this could happen. Never told him he'd get dunked so many times his ears would ring and he'd forget to close his mouth and breathe in gritty water, full of bugs. But they don't know who they're dealing with, this crowd. He won't quit. He'll keep on climbing back into that seat, no matter what, because that's why they pay him the big bucks and because those morons out there don't know shit. Not one of them knows how their skin smells when it starts to burn and they have never left their bodies, drifted, like he's drifting now, watching the people on the ground get smaller, smaller, slipping underneath a neon sign and past the rodeo announcer's booth, over the top rim of the Ferris wheel, on towards the stars, while somewhere down below, there is a brick house with a woman screaming and a man holding a small boy by the wrist and hissing, say it, say it now, you stubborn bastard, say you're sorry. No. Nobody knows a thing.

THE CLOWN HAS LOST his hat. His makeup's coming

off in patches and his face, beneath, looks startling-
ly smooth. How old is he? Who cares? The bystanders
have started chanting—*dunk him, dunk him*—stomping
and clapping in rhythm with the words. T.J. has not felt
this appreciated since the day he went to visit Sawyer's
school, before his first deployment. The principal held
an assembly in the gym and all the kids waved handmade paper flags. He does some arm circles, to loosen
up, and feels a sharp tug on his shirt.

It's Paige. She wants to tell him something. It looks
like maybe she is crying and—somewhere in T.J.'s
brain—he knows he needs to listen to his daughter, but
he can't. Not when he's on a roll. Not when the bullseye's pulling at him and the spectators are chanting, and
he's already decided his next throw is for those friends
whose names he'll never speak again, who were with
him on that day that never happened, nineteen months
ago.

"Dad?" It's Sawyer, this time. T.J. glances at his
son, wondering how the boy would interrupt him, at a
time like this. "Dad?" T.J. looks again, annoyed, and sees
that his two kids are holding hands. No doubt about it,
Paige is crying now. "Can we go home?" His son's voice
sounds determined and afraid. And T.J.'s raised arm
buckles as he sees his children, standing there. His kids.
He sees his kids. They're hurting, too.

THE SOLDIER'S LEAVING WITH one arm around each kid.
The dunk-tank crowd is breaking up. "Hey, where you
think you're going?" Caleb rasps, then spits. "Come back

here, Sarge, you chicken!" But he's gone. "Big chicken," Caleb coughs and shivers. "Bwok, bwok, chicken. Asshole. Pussy. Bwok, bwok, bwok."

Rocky looks up and grins at him—a rare, disturbing sight. He's missing his front teeth. "Yo kid, you should go take a break. Go get a corndog. Go warm up."

But Caleb, after coughing up more water, shakes his head. Why would he leave? He has the best seat in the house. Even with his molars chattering, he loves the carnival at night—the whirl and glitter and the sound of happy morons, wasting dough. From his seat, he can see the Doomed Titanic and the Matterhorn and on beyond these, in the fading hills, a strand of moving headlights on some highway: a parade of jeweled insects, heading home.

Monsters of the Deep

DURING THE LONG, HOT August after I turned ten, while our politicians argued over whether nuclear-head missiles were being aimed this way from Cuba, the citizens of my town worried mainly about who should keep the thousand-dollar grand prize in the fishing derby. A man who called himself E.C. Pardue produced a huge white sturgeon, twelve feet long, three-hundred-fifty pounds, by the official scale, and boasted that he'd slain the fabled monster of our lake. No one had actually seen him land this fish, and so my father, Big Jim, said it was a hoax; he said the sturgeon had been smuggled in from somewhere else, concealed in Pardue's Airstream trailer.

My father was a cherry farmer. We inhabited the same house on the same nine hundred acres where my great-grandparents once had turned the soil; he tended the same orchards which would someday be entrusted to the care of Little Jimmy, me, his only son.

Pardue, by contrast, came from parts unknown.

"HE'S A CONFIDENCE MAN," said my aunt Darlene, fitting a rubber ring into a Mason jar lid. "His license plates say California, but his boat is—pardon me." She edged around my mother, who was tending to a double boiler on the stove. They were making jam—a thing they did each year, for the Cherry Festival—and I was working on a pencil drawing, at the table. "His boat is registered North Carolina, of all places. And the address on his entry form was someplace in Alaska. Nome, maybe."

"That doesn't mean that he's a criminal, *per se*," said my mother, "just because he's not from here. You'd think we all would be relieved to have a rational explanation for our so-called monster, anyway."

"Creature," Darlene corrected her. "At our house, we say 'creature.' And Linnea, please don't tell me you believe he caught that fish here, in our lake."

"Why not?"

Darlene dropped a metal jar lid on the floor. It spun and clattered, till I picked it up. "For starters," said my aunt, "because the man's a charlatan. A swindler. A fake. Jimmy," she turned to me, a thing she often did when she grew weary of my mother's obstinacy. "Jimmy, you explain it. Tell her there aren't any sturgeon in this lake, for Pete's sake. Everyone knows that."

"But how can you be sure?" my mother countered. "Big Jim's always saying how a lake this size could hide all sorts of things."

Poor Darlene. A few wild strands had sprung loose from her carefully pinned hair, and beads of perspiration twinkled on her lip. "Because my Charles has seen the creature, don't forget. My husband knows a sturgeon when he sees one. And what Charles saw was no white sturgeon. Charles would know."

True story. 1954. My uncle Charlie, trolling in his

boat. Dawn, and the sky glows orange and pink behind the mountains, is reflected in the surface of the water. Then it shatters. Fish begin erupting on all sides—bait-size, pan-sized, too—all shooting straight into the air and flipping, twisting. Some of them land, gasping, in my uncle's boat. It looks, he thinks, as though the fish are trying to escape from something, and no sooner has this thought occurred to him than a great shadow looms, a dark stain spreading on the water, all around. Six feet away, the Evinrude is idling. Charlie grabs the oars. Too late. The boat rolls on a giant swell and he throws his weight to starboard, is confronted by a dripping cavern, lined with teeth. This is the end, my uncle thinks. He thinks the thing—whatever it may be—is going to eat him whole, the way the whale ate Jonah, but the boat rocks portside and the jaws hinge shut, incarcerating several hundred fish but not my uncle. He survives to tell the tale.

THERE WERE OTHER SIGHTINGS, that same year, but none of them from such a trusted source as Charlie. Former high-school quarterback-turned-coach, six-time winner of the fishing derby—my uncle had a reputation rivaled only by Big Jim's.

My mother said it was remarkable, under the circumstances, that Charlie got a good look at the monster, but he did. It was blue-black, torpedo-shaped, with four barbed fins and curving dagger-fangs. I'd made at least a dozen pencil sketches, based on my uncle's eye-witness report, and I thought some of them were pretty good, though I could never get the teeth exactly right.

After the jam had cooled, my mother funneled it into small jars, which Darlene wrapped with yellow cellophane. Their sale of cherry jam and baked goods at the 4-H auction helped to fund the fishing derby prize. "Jimmy," said my aunt. "I still don't understand why you're in here, with us. Why aren't you fishing with your dad?"

"He gets sick in the boat," my mother said. "I told you that."

"The lake is glass today. It isn't healthy for a boy his age to sit around inside. My boys have never stayed inside on a fine summer day."

In truth, my cousins had spent countless hours indoors, tormenting me. I supposed my aunt didn't know about the last time Mike and Bill came over, when they flushed my stamp collection down the toilet. Or the time before that, when they ripped up two of my new sketches, stuffed them in my mouth, and sat on me until I swallowed them.

Another thing Darlene didn't know was that my mother and I had already met E.C. Pardue, in person. We'd been on our way downtown, to pay a visit to the bookmobile, that morning. I carried my books in a sack: the usual assortment—Hardy Boys, a sci-fi almanac, and one called *Drawing Aliens and Monsters in 3-D*. My mother had a book tucked in her purse. Her purse was white and matched her gloves and hat. This was, remember, 1962. My mother always wore white gloves to town.

The road was just two lanes back then, with orchards

on both sides. There was a light wind, carrying the scent of fish and cherry trees and DDT. A fleet of sailboats, barely moving, on the lake. This lake of ours was thirty miles, from end to end, and sixteen miles across. It was the remnant of an inland sea, walled off by mountains, and therefore—according to my father's line of reasoning—the perfect habitat for organisms yet unknown to science, unclassified by phylum, order, genus.

We took the boardwalk, past the boat repair shop and past Frenchy's Diner, with its cardboard sign: *Contestants—Welcome! Wipe your Feet. Don't Clean Your Catch Inside.* I made my mother stop outside the Pioneer Museum, so I could see the rusted hulk of an old paddle-wheel steamboat called the Ivanhoe. This vessel had, in better days, been used for elegant excursions on the lake, back when the founders of our town arrived to chop down the primeval forests and plant cherry trees in evenly-spaced rows. Now it was beached in front of the museum, a landlocked shipwreck with a chain-link fence around it, to keep children out.

I laced my fingers through the chainlink, studied the dark holes where, once, there had been porthole windows. I'd been working on a drawing of this paddle-wheel. I needed to make sure I had the details right.

JULY 4, 1885. THE IVANHOE is on an afternoon cruise, several dozen genteel passengers on board. A perfect holiday, with champagne, sunshine and a string quartet that keeps the revelers waltzing till the stroke of six o' clock, when the sky changes, without warning, from azure to indigo. At the first sprinkling of rain, the gentlemen remove their frock coats, drape them round the shoulders of the ladies. Screams and laughter as a gust of wind knocks over music stands and scatters pages of a Mozart minuet across the deck. The rain becomes hail—the musicians scurry off like hunchbacks, trying to shield their instruments. The waltzers hold tight to each other as the dance-floor tilts and heaves. Only the captain—young McPherson, who later couldn't say a word for three whole days—is looking at the lake. Only the captain sees the shadow rise beneath the whitecaps and he's too perplexed to shout a warning until after the mysterious shadow rams the boat. The grand piano breaks loose from its moorings, slides across the deck and crashes through the guardrail, disappears. There's broken glass all over, from the smashed champagne flutes, and it cuts the feet of ladies in their dancing slippers, as the passengers swarm, panicked, towards the lifeboats.

Our man McPherson taps the foghorn three times, gives it three long blasts, then three more taps—the Morse code signal for distress. He's barely finished when the shadow surfaces again, a train-length body lolling there, amongst the waves. The ladies swoon; some gentlemen do, too. Much later, writing in his memoirs, the good captain will recall the monster's eyes. Those eyes, he'll say (and by the age of ten, I will have sketched at least three dozen pairs within the margins of my coil-ring exercise books) those eyes were twin coals, burning with malevolence.

•

WHILE WE WERE STANDING there, beside the fence, we heard a voice. "Did you ever wonder how far-gone they were?" Beside us was a tall man in a bone-hued linen suit, with a Panama-style hat pulled low over his blistered, sun-dark face. His shoulders slouched, as he stood looking at the boat, and his nose, viewed from the side, was long and aquiline.

"Who?" said my mother. "Where?"

"Your forefathers, aboard this paddle wheel." His voice was lazy, with a hint of Southern twang. "It sounds like they were pretty soused by the time your local Moby Dick showed up. No disrespect intended, by the way. I understand y'all have faith in monsters of the deep."

My mother crossed her arms in front of her. "I'm sure a few of them were sober. And besides, not everyone has faith."

He looked up, then, and staggered a few steps in feigned astonishment. "Why, this can't be! Surely I haven't met the only non-believer in this town?"

She flushed. "I'm sure I'm not the only."

The man removed his hat. Beneath, his hair was slicked back, somewhat thin on top. He was quite ordinary-looking, other than the fact that he was missing most of his left ear. "E.C. Pardue."

My mother took his outstretched hand, after a moment's hesitation. "Mrs. James Doyle. Pleased to meet you."

"Doyle? Not the James Doyle who runs the fishing derby? The one who's telling everybody I'm as crooked as a dog's hind leg?"

"The same."

"Well, well. Your husband may not be much of an angler, but I see he's to be envied, nonetheless." He leaned in, closer, and she pulled her hand away.

"That fish you caught," I blurted. "Is it really twelve feet long?"

"Oh yes," he said. "I've watched much better fishermen than I bring in some eighteen-footers, way up north. My sturgeon might have been a youngster, halfway-ripened, like yourself."

"How do you land a fish like that?" I asked. "How did you get it in the boat?"

He laughed. "I didn't. Saints alive, a catch that size would sink my little Crosby like a stone. No, son. After I set the hook I used a gaff—you do know what a gaff is, don't you, boy?"

I nodded. "Like a spear."

"That's right, except the one I used is called a flying gaff because it comes apart like this." He showed me, with his hands. "Spearhead. Handle. Rope connecting. A technique I learned amongst the Aborigines. They hunt the Great White from dugout canoes—how's that for courage? Anyhow, I got the gaff head hooked beneath my sturgeon's spine like so." He seized a handful of my shirt, between my shoulder blades, and shook me gently, side to side. "From that point, it was just a game to see who'd last the longest: me or him."

"You won."

"So it would seem, but not by much. Took me four hours to tow him in to shore. He was a fighter, I can tell you."

"Gosh."

"My husband," said my mother, evenly, "believes you brought that sturgeon in from someplace else."

I saw a dark look cross our new friend's face, but whether he was hurt or angry, I was at a loss to tell. He produced a white, embroidered handkerchief and sneezed into it. "Yes," he said, folding the handkerchief in neat, triangular quarters. "I've been informed of your husband's beliefs." He tucked the handkerchief back in his pocket, gestured at the book protruding from my mother's purse. "What's this?"

She took it out and handed it to him. It was a hardcover: *The Sea Around Us*. Rachel Carson. I expected our new friend to laugh, the way Big Jim did when he saw her borrowed titles lying open by the kitchen sink. She was the only mother I had heard of who read books while washing dishes, and the books she tried to read were often strange. My aunt Darlene read romance novels, ladies' magazines. No one I knew read Rachel Carson, then.

But Pardue didn't even crack a smile. He just flipped through the pages, silently, until he reached a photo of a palm tree-studded beach. "Ah, Bimini. I spent a fortnight there, in monsoon season. Rained so hard the animals were starting to pair up, but I still caught some beauties. Huge blue marlin. Swordfish. Sadly, most of them were apple-cored before I got them to the surface."

"Apple-cored?" I'd never heard the term.

"Yep. Mutilated. Eaten up by sharks, with nothing left between the head and tail but backbone and some tiny shreds of flesh. A crying shame."

"Is that what happened to your ear?" I asked. "Was it a shark?"

"Jimmy!" my mother said, but Pardue grinned.

"It's perfectly all right." He touched his fingers to the scar beneath his hat. "No, son. Jimmy, is that what they call you? James the second? No, my ear was severed by a colored gentleman, a witchcraft-doctor in Dobu. Nice man. But that's a story for another time."

"Yes," said my mother, reaching for her book. "Well. We really must be on our way. It was nice to meet you, sir, Mr. Pardue ."

"Madam. The pleasure was all mine." He spun his hat around his finger. "Say. Why don't the two of you come by the fairgrounds later, see the fish. They're holding the thing hostage in the Rotary pavilion. But you probably know that, since King James the First is the Grand Poo-bah of this fishing contest. Which reminds me, Jimmy, tell your pop he shouldn't feel too bad about my sturgeon. Even a blind hog finds an acorn now and then."

My mother pressed her lips together, but it was too late. I had already seen the corners of her mouth twitch up.

"Stop by my trailer, too," he said. "I've got some things might interest Junior here. Shark's teeth and other artifacts from Bimini. A pretty flute, carved from a narwhal's tusk. A large collection of old whaling implements from Tsarist Russia. Might interest you, yourself, Ma'am, since you're partial to marine biology." He gestured at the hardcover, now tucked beneath her arm.

"I'm afraid we won't have time for that, Mr. Pardue."

He shrugged and leaned down, hands upon his knees, face next to mine. Up close, he smelled like Brylcreem and live bait. "Hey listen, kid," he said. "You ask King James something, when you get home. Ask him how come so many people drown in this here lake and disappear. Ask him if he's ever wondered where their bodies go. Will you do that?" I nodded, mute. "Good boy. Then tell him this: sturgeon are bottom-feeders. Scavengers. That fish of mine got huge by eating human corpses, tell your daddy that."

"Jimmy." My mother yanked me by the hand. "Come on."

Pardue called after us, "I'm in the Boy Scout campground, if you change your mind. Third Airstream from the entrance, on your left."

As soon as we got home, I looked up "sturgeon" in *The Book of Knowledge*. In Volume XII, I found a photograph of Ernest Hemingway beside a giant fish—a sturgeon large enough to dwarf the smiling writer, by comparison, but much smaller than the monsters in my mind, the ones I sketched while other children were out doing whatever it was that other children did. Old Ernie's fish had jagged fins and a long body, shaped like a torpedo, which matched quite a few of the descriptions of our creature, though not all. By some reports, our monster was a serpent with sleek, iridescent humps that rose and fell above the waves in undulating rhythms. Such was the creature who'd revealed its sinuous curves at midnight to the crew of a small, chartered yacht, becalmed out in the center of the lake. After the serpent resubmerged, a sudden wind appeared and blew the yacht to shore. Or so the story went. I didn't know the men aboard that yacht. For all I knew, they might have been a pack of liars.

Beneath the photo was a block of text, wherein I learned these seven useful facts:

1) The sturgeon is a prehistoric species, nick-named "the Methuselah of fish." It has not evolved much in the past 200 million years,

2) The female sturgeon's roe is sold as caviar.

3) Unlike most other fish, the sturgeon has no teeth. (So Aunt Darlene was right. What Charlie saw could not have been a sturgeon). Because it has no teeth, the sturgeon swallows its prey whole. (The way the whale ate Jonah? Food for thought.)

4) Instead of teeth, the sturgeon has four tactile organs hidden underneath its wedge-shaped snout. These organs help it locate food on ocean floors and murky river bottoms, since the sturgeon is, primarily, a benthic feeder. (No mention of dead bodies here, unfortunately.)

5) Unlike most other fish, the sturgeon has no backbone.

6) Unlike most other fish, the sturgeon has no scales. Instead, it wears an armor of hard, interlock-ing bony plates.

7) The sturgeon can reach lengths of almost twenty feet and has been known to live one hundred fifty years. (Meaning, of course, that Pardue's fish

might possibly have been the thing that terrorized the Ivanhoe).

THE MONSTER TURNS, PREPARES to ram the boat a second time. Captain McPherson knows that all is lost. He sounds the S.O.S. once more and bows his head, like any good God-fearing Presbyterian, to pray. With his eyes closed, he doesn't see who fires the shot. He only hears it, echoing across the lake. When he looks up, he sees the monster, very much alive and foaming at the mouth. The next shot also misses, or perhaps it nicks the monster's dorsal fin, just barely. Whatever the case, the creature flicks its four-pronged tail and disappears. McPherson doesn't know who fired those rounds. Nobody knows. The hero is too humble to step forward. But because of the anonymous man's actions, everyone aboard the Ivanhoe survives. As does the monster, somewhere in the depths.

THAT EVENING, CHARLIE AND Darlene came over, with my cousins, Mike and Bill. I hid out upstairs, with my bedroom door locked, working on my latest sketch. I was satisfied with how the boat was turning out. I'd finished with the cross-hatch shading on the deck and had even managed an effect of water droplets, spraying from the paddle-wheel. As for the monster—he was just a pair of eyes beneath the shadow of a curling wave. I'd finished with the captain—his head bowed in prayer behind the wheel—and I was pleased enough with my conglomeration of scared passengers,

all dressed identically to the small, porcelain figurines
that waltzed inside our china cabinet, downstairs. The
only passenger I hadn't finished with was the one with
the gun, the one about to fire upon the monster. I had
already erased his face so many times the paper was beginning to wear thin.

After I'd been working on my drawing for an hour
or two, I heard my aunt and uncle saying their good-
byes. I heard their car, departing. And then I listened to
my parents in the kitchen, fighting. It was a rehash of an
argument I'd heard before. It went like this:

Big Jim: When I was his age, I went out for basket-
ball and Little League and wrestling.

Linnea: He tried sports. You saw how that turned out.

Big Jim: Because you let him quit. You shelter him.

Linnea: He's artistic, Jim. He's not like other kids.
And anyway, he gets straight "A's" in school.

Big Jim: He's something, that's for sure. Charlie says
he saw him on the dock this morning, standing
there. Just squinting at the water. Like a little old
man, lost in his own thoughts.

WHILE MY PARENTS FOUGHT, I kept on working, drawing and erasing until, bit by bit, my mysterious armed
passenger took form. When I'd first sketched him, he
had been a kind of Davy Crockett, grizzled, dressed
in furs and buckskin, but this time, when I'd finished
working, I'd discovered he'd become something entirely
different, he was not a mountain man at all. This time,
I'd drawn the hero beardless, with a long, hooked nose,

the top half of his face concealed by a light-colored, Panama-style hat.

The next day, when my mother and I went to town to run some errands and her footsteps strayed off the straight path between the crop insurance agent's office and the butcher's shop and through the arched and bannered fairgrounds gate, I didn't ask where we were going. I followed her across the midway, where some men in dirty dungarees were busy setting up the carnival rides. Outside the 4-H tent, a girl I knew from school was scrubbing down a calf. I licked my lips as we approached the Rotary Pavillion. Before we'd left, that morning, I had slipped my Brownie Starlet camera in my pocket, just in case, and now, I had a feeling something wonderful was going to happen. I had a feeling I was going to see something, at last, that matched the scale of my imagination.

I was wrong. The pavilion was a mess of folding tables, coffee cups, half-eaten pastries, and mimeographed copies of a Rotary Club bulletin. Along the back wall were some blocks of ice, in a long metal trough. The ice was melting, water leaked through rusted pinholes in the trough and ran in rivulets across the dirt-packed floor. The place smelled fishy, but the fish itself was nowhere to be seen.

"If you came to see the sturgeon, you're too late." We turned, and there was Aunt Darlene, framed in the doorway. She was carrying a coffee urn, the armpits of her flowered dress were ringed with dried white sweat. "We shipped it off this morning."

"Shipped it where?" my mother asked.

"Oh. Didn't Big Jim tell you?" Darlene set the urn down on the nearest table, breathing hard. "We sent it down to a biologist in Helena. He's going to cut it open, see what it's been eating. Tell us if it came from here or somewhere else."

My mother glanced at me, over her shoulder. I was standing by the trough, running my fingers back and forth across a block of ice that bore the imprint of a long, long tail. "What a shame," she said. "Jimmy would have liked to see it."

"Pity," Darlene agreed, clucking her tongue. "I'm surprised Big Jim didn't tell you. Still, it will be such a huge relief to put all this behind us. Jimmy, you should have been out with the boys this morning. My Charles got a thirty-pounder. I said to Mike and Bill: well, kids, looks like your dad reeled in a thousand bucks. Unless your Uncle Jim can go one bigger."

"You mean," my mother said, "unless your expert finds out that the sturgeon's really from this lake."

My aunt exhaled. She fixed a bobby pin above her ear and smoothed some wrinkles from the bosom of her dress. Her expression seemed to say that the fool-headedness of other women was a cross that she bore cheerfully, by virtue of her own, unflagging common sense. "Linnea." Her voice was slow and very calm. "That isn't going to happen, dear."

"How can you tell?"

"Well, for one thing, there's our fish biologist. His name is Rupert Henderson. He was Charles' college roommate. That's how I can tell."

•

THAT NIGHT, WHEN BOTH my parents were out, I left the house. My father had been first to leave, after an argument:

> Big Jim: Cheating? He's the one who's cheating. We're just trying to even up the score.
>
> Linnea: There's no proof he didn't catch that fish here, in this lake.
>
> Big Jim: And there's no proof he did. If there were sturgeon here, somebody in our family would have caught one, you can bet on that.
>
> Linnea: I can't believe you'd sink this low for money.
>
> Big Jim: This isn't about money. It's about our civic pride.

WHEN MY FATHER LEFT the house, the screen banged shut. It was the first time, in my memory, that I had ever heard him slam a door. My mother left a short time after. "I won't be very long. Get your pajamas on. Lock all the doors. If there's a fire, get out," she said. "Don't dilly-dally."

From the dormer window of my upstairs room, I watched my mother leave, on foot. My father had the car and anyway, she didn't drive. I watched until she turned the corner by our southeast orchard, started down the hill toward the main road. Then I rummaged through my dresser for an item I wore only once or twice a year. My swimming trunks.

I walked along the gravel road that led between our orchards, down the hill, right to the rocky shore. The lake, to borrow Darlene's term, was glass. Boats dozed on the horizon and a pair of mallards drifted past our dock. I kicked off my shoes. The colored rocks beneath my feet were warm from baking in the sun all day but the water, when I waded in, was cold as ever. I stood, quivering, while my toes turned white, then blue. This water came from melted glaciers—those unfortunates who found themselves immersed in it, too far from shore, never had to suffer very long. It was the cold that got them first—a fact that I found oddly reassuring.

1952: A TEENAGED COUPLE in a Chevrolet. They take the S-curve by the old hotel too fast and shoot straight over the cliff, into the lake. The boy gets out and swims to shore, leaving his girlfriend trapped inside. But when the rescuers arrive, to haul the Chevy out, the car is empty. Though the search will last a week, the girlfriend's body never will be found.

MY FEET WERE NUMB. I waded in a little further, to my knees. A school of minnows flitted round my calves. A sharp rock jabbed my left big toe. Our lake was deeper, in the middle, than the Yellow Sea. I'd never been in further than my waist.

The real reason I never went out in my father's boat: I was afraid. Not just of creatures still unclassified by science, though I was frightened of those, too, but of all things that dwelt beneath the surface, where the sunlight couldn't reach. In swimming pools I had no problem, but in our lake, I panicked, every time. I'd shut my eyes, so I wouldn't see the looming boulders, velvet-soft with scum, the shadows darting just beyond my thrashing hands. I'd hold my breath and try my hardest not to think of what was in the lake, besides myself, but all it took was one thin, rubbery tongue of seaweed, licking at my heel and I was gone. My muscles all went rigid and I'd sink, just like a stone.

1941: A POD OF naval ensigns from Annapolis are conducting training exercises on the lake. They're learning to use Sonar: a technology they hope will soon protect them from torpedoes, underwater mines. They're here because our mountains and our isolation are believed to be discouraging to foreign spies. But their Sonar picks up some perplexing signals. Something big is down there, something bigger, maybe, than a German sub. Yet the lake is deep, the ensigns are so inexperienced with Sonar; every time they get a reading, all the green blips on their screen dissolve and reconfigure in confounding ways. Their captain telegraphs word of these difficulties to his commander, back in Maryland, and his report is passed on through the ranks to the Rear Admiral, who is wrapped up in other things.

THE NEAREST SHORE WAS seven miles away. I waded deeper, wondered how long it would take to swim that far. I wasn't going to try it. I had no athletic aspirations and besides, I didn't want to die. I only planned to swim a little bit, to get out to the deeper water, past the dock. To prove that I could do it, that was all.

I took a few more steps. Now the water was chest-deep and I no longer felt the cold. It was as though I'd left my body; I was just a pair of eyes above the lake. I hovered, saw a skinny kid, about to swim. A brave kid, not unlike those Aborigines who hunted sharks from dugout boats. Only a few more steps and he'd be out where he could not touch bottom. One small push and he'd be somewhere he had never been before.

1949: A TURBO-PROP PLANE crashes, with a pilot and six smokejumpers aboard. None of the bodies are recovered, which is unsurprising, since the plane went down in flames, above the deepest section of the lake. Much stranger is what happens to the nets. Some of the nets, the ones the searchers use to drag the trench, are hauled back to the barge in tatters, full of large round holes.

WHEN I GOT BACK home, I found my father had returned. I stood beside the kitchen table, shivering, as his long shadow fell across me, but he didn't ask why I was dripping water on the floor. The only thing he said was, "Where's your mother?"

I don't know what time she came home that night. I was asleep, having a dream in which my mother and I were aboard the Ivanhoe, in formal dress. I was playing the piano. When the monster—which was not a monster, but a smiling, disembodied face—appeared above the waves, my mother drew a silver pistol from her purse and fired.

I was still pondering this dream at breakfast, the

next morning, when my aunt Darlene burst through our front door, breathless with the news that the nefarious Mr. Pardue was gone. He had skipped town, she told us, and get this: he had absconded with the thousand dollars, every penny (Lord only knows how he had found that money, stashed in such a secretive location, with the derby trophy, which was missing, too).

I never told my father—then or since—about the time my mother and I met Pardue. He couldn't have known, but still, I saw the way my father looked at her. I saw the series of emotions cross his face as she stared back at him across the breakfast table, without blinking. First curiosity, then doubt, enlightenment, followed by disbelief and rage and lastly, fear.

The fear remained there, in my father's eyes, all through that decade, while the world came to the brink of nuclear disaster and the booths at Frenchy's all filled up with long-haired, grubby kids. I saw it in his face when the first condominiums were built, along our boardwalk, when the first ski resort went in above our lake and when the men in suits came to our door to tell him he was no longer allowed to spray his orchards with his trusted pesticide. It lingered on throughout the war in Vietnam, while the Ivanhoe crumbled away to dust. It was still there in the next-to-last month of the Ford administration, when my father died.

I think it was the fear that brought me closer to Big Jim, at last, and not the fact that I had given up on drawing monsters. Fear was mine. It was the one thing I excelled at, as I came to know the time I tried to swim out past our dock, and lost my nerve. My vision blurred as I turned back toward shore, that summer night. Whatever it was that lurked beneath the waves could stay there. It was better not to know.

Fun with Color

NICOLE HAS NOT QUITE got the hang of walking in her new high heels. She limps along, complaining, hunched beneath the weight of our enormous bag. "No fair. How come I have to carry this?" she says, and I remind her that she's the apprentice. It's her job. Now, as we pass what used to be the foreman's office, boarded up, with "keep out" signs nailed to the door – she stumbles on the broken sidewalk, snags her hose on a sharp stem of knapweed growing through the chain-link fence.

"God damn."

"Nicole." We've talked about her language, more than once.

"Sorry," she says. "Sorry, sorry. I just hate these fucking shoes."

It's Saturday. We're targeting the company-owned houses by the mill. Nicole, as usual, is getting on my nerves: that high-pitched laugh of hers, her slouching walk. Each time we ring a doorbell, she forgets her lines but I am trying to keep my cool because Nicole, with all her flaws, is my last hope.

"Remember, chin up, shoulders back," I say, as we approach house two-o-six, identical to two-o-four and two-o-eight and all the other houses on this street. They date back to the early nineteen hundreds, when my great-great-uncle was a trim-saw operator at the mill. They're quaint, despite their missing shingles, tiny yards, despite the clothes lines strung from eave to eave. About half of them are boarded up now, and a few are even up on blocks, like junked cars, waiting to be moved. House two-o-six has no boards on the windows but the front porch is collapsing and the curtains are the color of bad teeth.

"Well, don't just stand there. Ring the bell, Nicole."

We listen to a dog barking inside until the door, at last, is opened by a grim-faced woman in a bailiff's uniform. Her Doberman is snarling at us from behind her legs.

"Good afternoon," Nicole says. We have practiced this. "Are you the lady of the house?"

The woman stares as if, poor thing, she's never thought about herself in quite those terms. She scratches her left bicep. "What you selling?"

"Beauty products," says Nicole. "First we invite you to a party. Then we try to sell you stuff." This isn't in the script. The woman tries to shut the door, but the Doberman makes a sudden lunge at us, between her legs and Nicole screams and almost topples off the porch. Our new friend drags the dog back by his collar, kicks him. Off he runs into the shadowy recesses of the kitchen, toenails sliding on the green linoleum.

I see my chance. While our potential customer's distracted, yelling at her dog, I ease myself into the house, insinuate myself into the narrow foyer until I'm close enough to see the clogged pores on her nose, when she turns back around. Oh, how I long to tell her all about exfoliating cleanser, cucumber astringent! It's too soon. Instead, I say, "We're representatives of Sunni Ray cosmetics and we're just thrilled to meet you . . . Valerie." I squint to read the nameplate on her chest.

"Hi, Val," Nicole waves from the porch. "It's nice to meet you. I like your tattoos."

"What my associate means to say is that we're here to ask you a few questions, Valerie."

I give Nicole the cue and she begins to stammer, "You . . . your regiment. Your . . . beauty . . . Val."

"We're here to chat with you about your beauty regimen," I intervene. Our Sunshine Handbook is quite clear about these situations. The Senior Sister's role, it says, is to educate the new initiate though good example and also, to correct her when she errs.

"So Valerie," I say, "how would you like to spend a few hours pampering yourself, experimenting with our new spring line?" Val's eyes, already small, contract to slits. I offer her a printed invitation to the party. "Let's be honest, Valerie. Wouldn't you love to spend a little time relaxing with some other girls? Just trying out new products, having fun with color?"

She blinks once, twice, and tries to shove me out the door. "Bring a friend," I say, bracing my hip against the jamb, "and you'll receive an eyelash curler as a gift." She's strong, but so am I. And then, just when it looks like I might lose this skirmish—my associate pipes up.

"Hey, you work at the courthouse, right?"

"Sure." Val is panting, now. "I'm a bailiff. Why?"

"I knew you looked familiar," says Nicole. "My boyfriend had to go there, just last month. He got a D.U.I. It wasn't actually his fault."

"Nicole," I say. If she were just a little closer, I could pinch her, surreptitiously. I've done it lots of times before. Instead, I draw my perfume spritzer from my purse, quick as a pistol, and start spraying our new fragrance, Debutante. The dim, cramped house fills up with scent, with undertones of citrus, sandalwood, magnolia. "Inhale," I say, blasting my spritzer all around. "Experience the romance of the antebellum South."

AFTER VAL SHUTS THE DOOR on us, we hit a losing streak. The next five houses all have trucks outside, but no one answers when we ring. We skip the last house on the street because I know the tenants there (a single dad, three sons) and continue past the front gates of the mill, without a word.

The gates are padlocked, naturally. The sign above them used to read: "Welcome to Harper Lumber—80 days without a lost-time accident." Now—thanks to some idiot with spray paint—it reads "200 days without a job."

A stray dog's sleeping in the loading yard where Nicole's boyfriend used to work. Lee Jay stacked plywood on the flat bed cars of trains bound for the coast. The trains still come; they rattle all the windows of the company-owned houses by the tracks, but they don't stop here anymore.

Two months ago, the roof of the production shop caved in beneath a heavy snowfall and so far, it doesn't look like there are any plans to fix it. The north wall of the shop is covered with graffiti, with lewd drawings, obscene words. Above these is a giant billboard: "Safety starts with 'us' and ends with Y-O-U!"

"I never understood that sign," Nicole says. "Safety doesn't end with 'u'."

When I don't answer, she says, "Are you mad at me?"

I draw a breath.

"You are. You're mad."

I stop. "Hold still." I take hold of her yellow scarf, which has somehow worked loose and is twisted up beneath her yellow blazer. "I am not mad." I give the scarf a tug. "I only wish that you'd remember Sunshine protocol, Nicole."

"Ow! Hey, you're choking me."

"I am not choking you. Next time, remember what our founder said. Decorum is the sign of inner strength."

"I can't breathe."

"Stop squirming. What a mess. Did you let Lee Jay tie your scarf again?"

"Uh-uh. My mom did it. God, these shoes are freaking torture."

"Sometimes we must make sacrifices for the greater good, Nicole. Like Sunni Ray. Her husband left her with three kids to feed, but did she let it ruin her attitude?"

"Um…"

"She did not. She devoted her entire life to helping other women reach new pinnacles of femininity. There." I smooth the wrinkles from her silk lapels. "Much better."

Nicole sets our bag of samples on the curb. She takes

off her left shoe and balances on her right leg, showing her slip. "Look, Avery! Look at this goddamn blister on my toe."

"I'd rather not."

"It hurts." She jams her foot into her shoe and snaps the waistband of her panty hose. "I'm sorry about Val. I know I shouldn't have told her about Lee Jay's D.U.I., but I thought, what the hell? I mean, she wasn't really the Sunni Ray type anyway."

"The type?" I'm shocked. "Oh, you're a snob, Nicole. Any woman can be taught to let her inner beauty shine. And I'll tell you what: there's not a female on this earth who doesn't crave a little bit of glamour in her life."

DON'T THINK I HAVEN'T wondered what our founder, Sunni Ray, would have to say about this place, about Nicole. According to the Handbook, new recruits are to be cultivated from amongst one's inner circle of acquaintances: from bridge clubs, philanthropic groups, salons—from any of those places ladies congregate in leisure hours. The problem is that I don't have too many close friends, nowadays, and there's no bridge club in this town.

Nicole is not an excellent apprentice, I admit. It isn't just that she forgets the script and mispronounces words like non-comodogenic and exfoliation. No, it's her attitude that troubles me. She coasts through life as though she's perfectly content to go on living in her little house, with Lee Jay and her mom and her four-year-old son Chase—who isn't even Lee Jay's offspring, incidentally.

"You need to think about the future," I once told her, when her motivation seemed especially low. "You have to ask yourself, where will I be when all my youthful charms are gone?"

WE GET BACK TO Nicole's at two o clock, an hour before the party's supposed to start. The yard looks better than it usually does, which isn't saying much. Someone has picked up most of Chase's plastic toys, but left the lawn unmowed. "I thought we were going to get this fixed." I indicate the gaping hole in the screen door.

"I tried. I asked Lee Jay to take care of it but he says it's better this way. This way, he doesn't have to get up to let Chase go in and out."

Lee Jay isn't in his usual chair, in the front room, but he is home. I can hear the television going in the bedroom. We find Brenda in the kitchen, finishing a cigarette.

Nicole says, "Mom, you're not supposed to smoke in here. Remember?"

Her mother rolls her eyes and stubs her cigarette out on a saucer. "What took you two so long?" For twenty-five years, Brenda did the payroll at the mill. If there's one person I can't stand, it's her.

"We walked for miles," Nicole says. "See my blister? Oh, Chase, sweetie. I thought you were napping." Her son is standing by the fridge in Tweety Bird pajama pants, no top. He has a plastic toy beneath one arm.

"Sneaky," Brenda says. "I knew he had that airplane in his bed with him."

"It's not a plane," the kid says. "It's a spaceship."

Nicole says, "He didn't sleep at all? Damn. He gets cranky when he skips his nap."

"Well, don't blame me," says Brenda. "You're the one bought him that stupid plane."

"Spaceship!" Chase yells. "It's a spaceship! Duh!"

"That's it." Nicole says. "You're going back to bed this minute, mister." Her son runs down the hallway, barricades himself inside the bathroom.

"He's spoiled," says Brenda, while Nicole pleads with her son through the closed door. "Believe me, he doesn't pull that crap when I'm in charge. How long's this hen party of yours supposed to last?"

"It's hard to say." I'm busy opening the windows in the kitchen and the front room. "A couple hours, at least. Depending on how many guests show up." I spritz a little Debutante around the living room and fluff the cushions on the brown plaid couch. At least Nicole is not a smoker anymore. She gave up nicotine and alcohol before her swearing-in. All new consultants have to pledge to keep a neat house, wholesome body and clean mind. Caffeine is allowed, in moderation. "Of course, we don't expect you'll want to stick around during the party, Brenda. You must have other things to do."

"Not really." The phone rings.

"That's probably one of your guests," says Brenda, drumming her fingers on the table. "Calling up to tell you they're not coming."

I'VE BEEN IN THIS business since last August, since about three months after the mill shut down. The closure wasn't a surprise. My husband's worked there since he finished high school, and the two of us have seen it all—a three-month furlough here and there, layoffs, suspended operations, strikes. We didn't panic when we heard the company had filed for bankruptcy. "Don't worry," Ty said, "rumor is they've found a buyer. Some outfit from Canada."

My first week on the job I got more sales leads than my Senior Sister, Janice. Janice said that she could tell I had a gift, and sure enough, I earned my stripes before Thanksgiving, record time. There's no telling where I'd be right now if the economy was good. In past years, when the mill shut down, our laid-off men could just drive to the city and sign on with the construction crews down there. Not anymore. Down in the city, things are just as bad as here. My sales are dwindling, yes, but I stay positive. I'm putting all my energies into recruitment and I'm proud to say I've mentored four different apprentices, already—although none of them have lasted long enough to earn their Sunshine stripes. That's why I'm being extra-patient with Nicole.

Whenever a new sister earns her stripes, her mentor gets five thousand points and a gold-plated brooch, shaped like a sun. Points help you earn incentives, understand. Like the carnelian earrings, just three hundred fifty points. Or the yellow Oldsmobile: one hundred thousand. Our regional convention's in July—too soon for me to earn the car, but I don't care. I'm only interested in one prize. No matter what, I'm going to win the trip for two to Paris, France.

I've never been to Paris, though I've researched it

online. In Paris, all the women wear good clothes and go to operas and ballets. In Paris, I can tell you this: nobody's screen door has a hole.

THE FIRST GUEST TO arrive is Fay, who used to operate a forklift at the mill. Nowadays, she works the deli counter at the grocery store.

Rosemary rings the doorbell while Fay's busy eating deviled eggs, having already polished off one whole tray of pimento sandwiches. I've always wondered how Fay stays so thin.

Denise is last. She's almost half an hour late. Denise's husband, everybody knows, is off in North Dakota, working in the oil fields, getting rich. Today, while I am busy setting nineteen jars of nail enamel on the table, Denise starts flaunting the designer purse her husband sent her, as a gift.

"What makes you think it's real?" asks Brenda.

"I can tell," Denise says. "Touch the leather. Silky smooth."

"Feels fake to me."

"So did you hear the Crandall girl had twins?" asks Rosemary. Rosemary was a bank teller for years. She still knows everyone in town. "Twin boys," she says. "Identical."

"Aw, sweet," Denise says, yanking her purse back from Brenda. " I didn't realize that Stephanie was married."

"Well, she's not."

"Ha! What'd she name the kids?" says Brenda. "'Oops' and 'Dammit'?" and the way she laughs, you'd think she didn't remember why her own daughter quit high school, senior year.

"Speaking of baby boys," says Rosemary, turning from Brenda to Nicole, "where's yours?"

"He's in our room," Nicole says. "Watching T.V. with Lee Jay. I promised both of them a Tootsie-roll if they stay in there till we're done."

We start with manicures. Nicole does well. She goes through the cuticle-remover demonstration by herself, with only a few prompts. She has some difficulty with the color palette, which is no big deal. Apprentice sisters aren't required to have the palette memorized until their third review. Myself, I had it memorized the first week—I don't mean to brag. The secret is to use a melody. For example, for the nineteen shades of nail enamel, I made up a ditty to the tune of Good King Wenceslas. Etruscan Mist, Clandestine Kiss, Gilded Tiger Lily . . . it goes on, of course—that's just the start. I made up other songs to teach myself the lip shades and the eye shades and the fourteen tints of Sunny Ray foundation. I used to sing them all the time. This was in early fall, when Ty still left the house most days, so I had privacy. I'm not about to teach Nicole this trick, however. Some things, she'll have to figure out herself.

Nicole paints Fay's nails Aphrodite Red, but Fay won't keep her hands clear of the chip bowl long enough for them to dry, so she ends up with salt stuck to her manicure. Denise insists on doing her own nails. She asks, as she applies a basecoat of Plum Shimmer, "What's your hubby doing these days, Avery? I haven't seen him in a while."

"Oh, keeping busy," I say. "Actually, he's thinking about going back to school. One of those online universities."

"Well, good for him." Denise gives me a patronizing smile. "That's great."

"Yeah, I'm thinking about going back to school myself," says Rosemary. "If I can get a loan." She holds her new blue fingernails up to the light. "There's this new correspondence program I found out about. Eleven months and you learn how to be a certified mortician." The others all guffaw but I can tell that Rosemary is serious. "What, what?" she says. "They give you a diploma and all that. Eleven months and you're in business."

"No!" Nicole says, giggling. "Shut up."

"Oh, go ahead. Make fun of me. Say what you want, the job's recession-proof."

"I'm sorry, Rosemary." Nicole covers her mouth.

"Sure, go ahead and laugh," says Rosemary. "We'll see who's scoffing next year, when the mill's still closed. A lot of people think the job is only about handling dead bodies, fluid extraction and the like, but that's just one small part of it. Mostly, it's a people job, the same as yours. It's about building personal relationships."

"Ew!"

"You just say that because you're young, Nicole," says Rosemary. "Just wait."

"Excuse me." Fay reaches past her, for the ham puffs.

"Avery," Denise leans towards me, stroking her leather purse like it's a cat. "I must say I'm a bit surprised your man won't try the oil-fields. I can understand, in Lee Jay's case.

Lee Jay's a dad. But you and Ty don't have a family yet."

"We are a family," I tell her. "Ty and me. We built our house all by ourselves, with our own hands." That shuts her up. I start clearing off the table, putting lids on all the polish jars.

WHEN I WIN MY trip for two, I'll take my husband, Ty, of course. It'll be his first time on a plane.

There might be some men in my husband's lineage with no connection to the timber industry, but you'd have to go back pretty far. His great-great-uncle trimmed logs from the time he landed in this country, up until the day he died. Ty's great-grandfather started at the mill at age fifteen, was joined, in time, by his three sons—all crossband layers—and a pair of nephews—truss assemblers, both. Ty's older brother worked the planer until he moved up to quality control and Ty's cousin was his right-hand man, assistant supervisor of production, twenty years. We used to joke that if we ever had a son, the baby would have sawdust in his veins, instead of blood.

Last January, Ty went to a meeting at the Union Local. Some guy from Washington D.C. was there to talk about a federal retraining program. When Ty came home, he didn't bother taking off his coat. He just sat down. "They want to teach me how to repair furnaces and air conditioners."

"Oh, good."

He shook his head. "That isn't what I do."

•

AFTER THE MANICURES, WE do the facials and then makeovers. While Nicole is demonstrating how to blend concealer, I unwrap my twelve-by-sixteen portrait of our founder and prop it on the coffee table.

"This photograph was taken a few months before she passed away," I said. "It has not been retouched in any way. How old would you guess Sunni was, from her appearance?"

Silence. "Don't be shy. Would you say fifty-five? Or sixty, tops?" I pause strategically. The only sound is the soft pop of a lid detaching from an eyebrow pencil.

"What if I told you she was eighty-seven? Yes, you heard correctly. Observe the skin around her eyes, the elasticity. This shows the value of a daily moisturizing regimen."

"You sure she wasn't dead already?" Brenda asks. "She looks like someone Rosemary would like to get her hooks into."

With Brenda, often the best strategy is to pretend you didn't hear. "If you follow Sunni's plan," I say, raising my voice above the snickering, "I guarantee that you will see results. Ninety-six percent of our customers report looking younger within thirty days."

"True story," Nicole says. "Just last week, I got carded buying smokes, and I'm almost twenty-two!" She looks at me. "The pack was for my mom."

"Hey, that reminds me," Brenda interjects. "If anybody sees an ashtray, holler. My beloved daughter hid them all before this shindig started."

Denise stands up. "I'm sorry, girls. I have to move

around some or my knees lock up."

"Well, that makes two of us," and Brenda heaves herself up off the couch, stretches both arms above her head.

Rosemary's scowling at the catalog. "How come there's no prices in this thing?"

"Our products are one-hundred percent natural," I say, "and have never been tested on animals. Sunni Ray loved animals." I'm about to talk about her interest in endangered primates when I'm startled by the pitter-patter of small feet. Chase takes a lap around the living room, colliding with the coffee table, making Sunni's portrait crash face forward on the rug.

"Chase, sweetie," says Nicole. "Be careful, please!" He pauses for a moment, long enough to snatch my portrait of the founder and run off with it, down the hall.

I look at my apprentice. She's pretending she didn't see.

"Well, holy crap," says Brenda. "Those Vienna sausages are salty. Who else wants a beer?" Four hands shoot high into the air, including, I am sad to say, Nicole's.

Chase isn't in the bathroom, nor the room he shares with Brenda, which means he must be in the other bedroom. I don't knock. I'm so upset that I've forgotten about Lee Jay, who is lying on the bed, watching TV He's fully dressed—thank God for that—but looks as if he hasn't shaved in days. "Excuse me," I say, opening the closet. I start rummaging around, digging through piles of the laundry, looking for the little boy. Lee Jay doesn't seem to mind. He's absorbed in some TV show where celebrities go shopping for new homes. "Hey, check it out," he says, without taking his eyes off the TV. "This one has fourteen bathrooms. That's badass."

Chase isn't in the closet, so I get down on the linty carpet, lift the corner of the bedskirt. Sure enough, a pair of feral eyes shine back at me. "Come here," I say. "Give me the picture. That's a good boy." When I reach for him, the kid scoots backwards, further underneath the bed. I don't want to follow him—the floor beneath the bed's a mess of dustbunnies and bottlecaps—but I can't afford another portrait, so I crawl, commando-fashion, trying not to think about how much it's going to cost to have my outfit dry-cleaned, after this. "Come on. Remember what your mom said. Don't you want that Tootsie Roll?"

Above us, Lee Jay's talking to the television. "That's just lame. Who needs a drawbridge anymore?"

I keep my eyes on Chase. He hasn't budged. I count to three inside my head, then lunge at him and grab my portrait, not before he sinks his teeth into my hand and breaks the skin.

"You little brat!"

"Hell, yeah," says Lee Jay, as I edge past the bed, clutching my portrait. "Check it out. It's got a mini-golf course. I'd buy that."

I lock the bathroom door and hold my hand under the tap until the bleeding stops.

WHEN WE ARRIVE IN Paris, France, the first place we will go is to the Louvre. Ty doesn't know if he's the type for art museums, but I tell him he'll love it, wait and see.

If not, I guess he can go fishing while I'm at the Louvre. They have a river there. It's called the Seine.

WHEN I FINALLY LEAVE the bathroom, having done my best to sponge the dusty smudges from my blazer, I hear laughter coming from the living room. Denise is talking. "Certainly, you may find cheaper products," she is saying, in a strained falsetto, "but the thing you have to ask yourself is am I worth it? Am I worth this forty dollar lip gloss? Will it make my inner goddess shine?" More laughter and a slow prickling of perspiration underneath my scarf as I realize what's going on, in there. They're mocking me.

In all my months as a consultant, this has never happened. Never. I ask myself what Sunni Ray would do, but there is nothing in our Handbook about dealing with backstabbing clientele. I could go back into the bathroom but the bathroom smells like mildew and besides, I'm not a coward.

So I march down the hallway and stand in the entrance to the living room, arms crossed. They keep on talking. They don't notice me. They're all half-drunk already, I suppose.

"Lord, she's a bossy little thing," Denise is saying. "How do you put up with it, Nicole?"

"I tell you what," says Brenda. "It was me, I'd show her where to put her sunshine protocol."

"I know." Nicole is peeling off the label on her bottle. "I know Avery is strange. But she's been helping me, okay? I know what people say about me. I just want to show them I can be someone. Sunni Ray said women have to take charge of their destinies. Or something like that, I forget."

"Oh, Nicky. Honey." Brenda's voice is gentler than I've ever heard it. "Honey, there are better ways. Besides, your life isn't so bad."

"That's right," Denise nods. "I've seen worse."

"It's like my mother always said," Fay wipes a bit of crab dip from her chin. "You get what you get and you don't throw a fit."

I clear my throat and everybody jumps. Nicole looks up at me, then looks away. Her face turns Cherry Blossom Pink, as well it should.

"What's the matter with you people?" I advance into the room stand beside a cabinet containing bowling trophies, Zippo lighters and a cuckoo clock, shaped like a tree, the words "Las Vegas" rhinestoned on the trunk. "Look around you," I say, gesturing at the dark wood paneled walls. "Look around. Is this really all you want?"

Denise studies her brand-new manicure, the ingrate. No one speaks. "Nicole," I say, at length. "Nicole?"

Her face turns darker pink—a shade away from Vintage Valentine—but my apprentice still won't look at me. Six weeks of training and now all she can do is rip a beer label into confetti in her lap. "Nicole?" I say again. The cuckoo clock chirps four o'clock. Then all is quiet—except for Fay, still crunching Triscuits on the couch.

"Fine." I start picking up the product samples, packing them into the bag. "Terrific. Be content with what you have, Nicole. Just don't blame me when you wind up all alone, someday, covered with wrinkles, liver spots, and cellulite."

"Oh, I won't be alone," Nicole says softly. "I'm a mom."

WHEN I GET HOME, I dump the tote-bag in the closet. I pry off my heels and set them next to Ty's best pair of steel-toed boots, now gray with dust.

The TV's blaring in the den but no one's watching. On the coffee table is a dinner plate, encrusted with the dried remains of a beef casserole I made three days ago. I pick it up and take it to the kitchen. My husband's sitting in the breakfast nook, still in his robe.

"Hey," he grins. "How was the big event?"

"Don't ask." I start to fill the sink.

"What happened to your suit?"

"I told you, I don't want to talk."

"Well, I've got something that should cheer you up." He takes a velvet-covered box out of the pocket of his robe. "Here. Open it."

Inside is a gold bracelet with an opal, fat and lustrous as the full moon in my favorite photo of the Eiffel tower. It's beautiful. "What's this?" I say, when I can finally speak.

"You like it? Eighteen karat gold. I wanted to surprise you. You deserve—"

"Ty, how much did this cost?"

"They had a payment plan." He shrugs. "I knew you'd like it. I just thought, why not?"

"Why not?" My hands are shaking so much I can

hardly hold the box. "Why not? Did you know we got another warning from the power company? Do you realize the grocery store won't take our checks? Our names are on a list there, right where everyone can see."

Ty looks like he's been punched. I ought to stop. "The mill is done," I say, under my breath. "There is no buyer. Everyone knows that."

PARIS: WORLD CAPITAL OF haute couture. Also, the city of romance. While there, a couple might choose to eat pastries on their hotel balcony and watch the children in school uniforms, below. Later, they'll feed pigeons in the park and when the sun sets, he and she will kiss beneath a streetlamp like two people who remember how they once were, how they radiated hope.

Fourteen Tips for Selling Real Estate

TIP #1: Make sure your house has an appealing smell. Bake cookies, light a fragrant candle, place fresh bowls of potpourri in every room.

"THERE'S AN ODOR IN here," says the agent, Trish, her high heels clacking on the green linoleum. "Something smells odd. I don't know what it is."

"Mothballs?" says Jack, while thinking, "Death? Decay?"

"No. It's something else. But if you do have mothballs, you should get rid of them, pronto. If there's one scent that turns potential buyers off, in my experience, it's mothballs. Blech."

"We don't have any," Jack says. "I was joking."

"Oh," says Trish. "Well, there's an odor, anyway. I don't know. Medicine, maybe."

"Medicine, yes. We do have lots of that."

TIP #2: Lighting matters! Before a showing, open curtains and raise blinds in every room. Floor-lamps can help create a warm, inviting atmosphere.

FRIDAY MORNING. JACK IS down at Wal-Mart for the second time this week. He's stuck in line behind a crew of wildland firefighters, who are in there buying candy bars and smokes and cold drinks. Jack himself is buying lightbulbs, much to his chagrin.

The crew is from the reservation, so Jack gathers from the words embroidered on their jackets: Blackfeet Nation Hotshots. Most of them have yellow hats beneath their arms and one, a very tall young man in front of Jack, is wearing his. The tall kid's arms are loaded down with chips and jerky and he wears the kind of knee-high boots that used to give Jack blisters, back when he was fighting fires. Jack knew some guys from Browning then, and he considers asking this tall boy if he knows any of those long-lost friends, but then Jack thinks: why bother? Nobody knows anyone, these days.

The clerk apologizes. She's a girl about the same age as Jack's daughter—fifty-something, but much shorter than his Lisa, with a rounder face. "I'm sorry for the wait, sir. That's the third crew we've had through here, on my shift, I kid you not. They've pretty much wiped out the carbonated beverages aisle, but you can't blame them, can you, in this heat?" She turns a light-bulb over, looking for the bar-code. "How many of these have you got there, ten?"

"Eighteen," says Jack.

"Eighteen. That's a lot of bulbs."

"Tell me about it," Jack says, opening his wallet. "Suddenly, we've got to have new light bulbs. Our old ones won't do. We've got to replace them all, the realtor says."

"Realtors," sniffs the clerk. She stares off, through the plate glass windows, at the smoky sky. "You know what we need? Wind. We need a good strong wind to clear the air."

Jack is silent, smoothing out the creases in his dollar bills. Forty-six years, he labored for the forest service, in the woods and later, from behind a big oak desk. Forty-six years, and still the general public's ignorance of wildfire is astonishing to him. Wind, indeed. She ought to be ashamed.

Crossing the parking lot, his damp shirt sticking to his ribs, Jack sees the fire crew, standing in a semicircle by their van. The men are eating, chatting, making jokes, as though they are impervious to degrees Fahrenheit. The smoke lies heavy all around, dusking the noon sky, making haloes around streetlights. The mountains have all vanished and the sun is nowhere—just a high red haze.

He checks his watch. Adele has been alone for thirty minutes. Not too long—she's probably still asleep, Jack thinks. But he starts walking faster, just in case.

TIP #3: Do your best to keep in step with trends in home décor. Watch home design shows on TV, read decorating magazines. Buyers are drawn to homes with a contemporary look.

BEFORE THE FIRES, JACK used to take his wife on walks, twice daily, which exhausted him. Adele walks fast, she always has. Their children used to tease her that she'd never owned a pair of shoes she couldn't hike five miles in, should the need arise. On their walks around the neighborhood, Jack begged her to slow down, not just so he could catch his breath, but also so that he could point out landmarks and remind her of the names of neighbors, people they have known for years.

But since the fires got started, what they mostly do is sit down in the basement, where it's cool, and watch TV. Today, they're watching *Jeopardy*. Adele crochets. Jack marvels at the quickness of her hands, covered with knotty veins, but just as agile, now, as they were when she was twenty-one and teaching school. Adele knows every answer for "State Capitals," as well as "Great Composers." She even nails the final question, under "Sixteenth-Century Explorers" ("Ponce de Leon", she says, without dropping a stitch). This makes Jack proud and also fills him with an all-encompassing despair.

Tip #4: Never underestimate the power of curb appeal. Some well-placed shrubs and a newly painted door can transform your place from ho-hum to sensational.

JACK SWEEPS THE PORCH. He gathers up the fine white ash and dumps it in a bucket, over layers of coffee grounds and eggshells. He'll use it later, on his roses.

He checks the mail—three bills, two advertisements for prescription drug plans, an invitation to his fifty-eighth reunion—and stuffs it all back in the box, just as the sky shrills and a turboprop plane, painted red and silver, like a toy—makes a low pass overhead. So low Jack almost ducks. He half-expects the plane to clip the tallest ponderosas in the gulch across the street, but it clears them, is absorbed into the haze.

The nearest fire complex is several miles away, but sometimes, when Jack checks the mail, he discovers tiny burnt twigs on the sidewalk, charred white threads that crumble at his touch. He's seen, on television, that there are crews, now, from eleven states, fighting the blazes on the ground and from the air. It's the worst season in nearly fifty years, since back when Jack himself was on a ground crew, learning how to build a line.

The smoke is bad enough—the suffocating smell, the taste of it—and the sky, which is cement-gray, toxic orange at dawn, but it's the noise that finally wears a person down. The fire planes flying over, night and day—refurbished bombers, helitankers—their sound reminds Jack of newsreel clips they used to show when he was young, too young to join the big boys overseas. No, this is nothing like that war, not really—forests can grow back—but still, it wears a person down. It's not, as even Trish admits, the optimal environment for selling homes.

Tip #5: If you have a wife with Alzheimer's disease, attempt to keep her in the basement, out of sight.

Adele is downstairs, playing the piano. It's a minuet by Mozart, one she learned when she was nine years old. Her hands move up and down the scale; the decades roll back like arpeggios. She hears her mother on the stairs and remembers that she's not supposed to practice while her baby brother is asleep. She drops her hands into her lap and turns to tell her mother that she's sorry, but her mother isn't there, where she should be. Instead, there's some old man she doesn't know. He's watching her.

TIP #6: Remove your personal memorabilia from the house. We want potential buyers to imagine themselves living there, not you.

ANOTHER FRIDAY. JACK IS emptying the china cabinet—something he's been putting off for months. He takes the porcelain figurines out first, wrapping each one in newspaper before he lays it in the box. Here's a curly-headed shepherd, with a lamb. Here's a long-necked dancer with a pigeon resting on her fingertips. A pigeon? No. That bird must be a dove. Christ, why do women always love this crap?

Some buyers are coming to see the house, at last. They haven't had a showing for three weeks. Trish says not to worry, these things happen, particularly at the height of wildfire season. It only takes one buyer, Trish says, which is all the more reason to take care of unfinished jobs, like this. She's been nagging him about the china cabinet since before they planted the for-sale sign in the yard.

He finds a pair of salt and pepper shakers, shaped like ducks. Also the mug Tom made at Boy Scout camp, one year. A bighorn sheep, carved out of wood—Adele bought this on their honeymoon, in Glacier Park. He ought to put it all in the garage sale pile, thinks Jack. They won't have room for any of it, where they're going.

The cabinet is empty, now, except for dust. Jack gets a roll of paper towels and starts wiping off the shelves. The cabinet's an heirloom, brought out west by covered wagon. It belonged to someone's great-grandmother—Jack's, maybe. Or else Adele's. Whose was it? Damn, he can't recall. His wife would know, or would have, at one time. He should have listened while he had the chance.

His first chore finished, Jack moves on to the front room. The wall above the couch is full of family pictures, all of which need to be taken down. Jack takes down Lisa in her Snow White costume, lays the photo in a box, then does the same with Tom, playing a plastic ukulele, and Tom, much older, holding his first child. After the first few, it gets easier. He scarcely glances at the pictures as he lifts them from their hooks and soon the wall above the couch is bare, or nearly so.

The last remaining picture is from 1950. It's Adele, inside the one-room schoolhouse, where she started her career. Children of every size are seated, two to a desk. Girls on the left side of the room, boys on the right. The boys have crew-cuts, all of them, which make their ears look huge. The girls have braids and knee socks, pleated skirts. Adele herself is pretty in a Fair Isle sweater, pleated skirt, her hair in geometric coils around her face. Pretty yet fierce, with eyes as bright as the nocturnal animals Jack's father used to trap to make a living (if you could even call it that, a living). Fierce, yes. Jack smiles. Pity the child who showed up late for Miss McDonnell's class.

Jack puts the photo in the box, then takes it out

again, for one last look. In the background of the photo there is something he has not noticed before. It's a list of words, up on the chalkboard, in Adele's impeccable DeNealian:

1. harvest
2. cider
3. fathers
4. mothers
5. churn
6. butter
7. beautiful
8. horses

SHE'D ONLY BEEN AT her new job three weeks before Jack found a way to meet her. Much to the envious consternation of his buddies at the Jackalope Saloon, he'd conned his way into a job delivering firewood to the school, a quarter cord per week. It took six months before she'd smile at him, another two before she'd say hello, though Jack could feel her eyes on him, sometimes, when he was splitting wood.

His pals down at the Jackalope all said that she was much too good for him, and he agreed. Now, looking at the picture, Jack recalls a Christmas party that he took Adele to, one time, at the Kinley's. By this time, they were practically engaged, and yet she'd slapped his errant hands beneath the blanket they shared on the sleigh ride under the blue stars, slapped him until he ached all over and when the ride was done, he'd tumbled off the sleigh, worn out by lust and too much home-brewed cider and the jarring gait of Dermott Kinley's huge moon-dappled Percherons. Two hired hands were there to help him up, holding Jack underneath his arms. They nearly died of laughter when he staggered off to vomit in the newly fallen snow.

Jack hangs the photo back up on the wall. Why should he hide all traces of their past? The hell with Trish. It's not her house. But then he thinks: it only takes one buyer, and he puts the photo face-down in the box.

TIP #7: Don't forget, the kitchen is the most important room. Ask your realtor for ideas on how to give yours sparkle and pizzazz!

ADELE HAS LEFT THE fridge door standing open, once again. Jack closes it, then wipes the scattered bread-crumbs from the counter, trying to contain his irritation. She used to be so tidy, all the time.

The clock above the stove says one o' clock. Trish isn't supposed to show up, with her clients, till half past three, which means Jack has about an hour to kill before he needs to get Adele up, dressed, and in the car. He'll take her to the mall to walk around. She likes the mall; she doesn't get upset there, usually. It hasn't changed that much, in thirty years.

He checks inside the oven. Clean, of course. Nobody's used the thing in months. It still works perfectly, though Trish—with her usual zest for squandering Jack's pension—has suggested that he ought to buy a new one. No, worse than that, she thinks Jack should replace all of the appliances. She told him this last month. "That color," she said, "is a major ick."

"A major what?" said Jack, and he had wanted to tell Trish that his wife had picked them out, back when they built the house. Adele had picked that color— "harvest gold," not because it was in vogue, but because she liked the way it matched the foothills, east of town. But he's not willing to discuss his wife with Trish, so he told her, instead, about the two-room cabin he'd grown up in, where his mother fed and clothed four kids without the aid of one appliance—gold or otherwise—because the power-lines did not extend that far from town, back then. He stopped himself before the part about how he and his three sisters had to take turns hauling water from the well. He could tell, from the forced way Trish was smiling at him, she had heard all this before.

TIP #8: Communication counts! Remember that your real estate professional is always there to listen to your questions and concerns.

ON SUNDAYS, LISA CALLS. Today she says, "Have you been eating, Dad?"

"Of course."

"Tom says Mom didn't cook at all, the last time he was there."

"Well, she gets frustrated. But we're doing fine. I actually know how to fix some stuff."

"Like what, Dad? Corned beef hash? You can't subsist on corned beef hash, you know."

"We're doing fine. How are the girls?"

"They're great. I wish your house would sell. No offers yet?"

"Not yet. It's—you know—the economy, and this damn smoke. The fires are making things a little difficult. But Trish is bringing some clients by to see the place, the day after tomorrow."

"Good. That's good. I saw your fires on our nightly news. They're not too close?"

"No, no. We're not in danger. Don't you fret. Though lately I've been wishing they'd just let them burn, you know? Just let them burn this place right to the ground. Save us a lot of hassle, don't you think?" He laughs. His daughter doesn't.

"Dad."

"What?"

"Do you want me to come out there?"

"No. I mean, not unless you want to."

Silence.

TIP #9: If you are old, please make your presence inconspicuous. Potential buyers do not like to be reminded of their own mortality. No one cares that you were once considered something of a catch.

ADELE IS FOLDING LAUNDRY in the front room. Halfway through, she stops, aware of a faint smell. Something is burning. Wood. Well, naturally, it's wood-smoke, from the corner stove. That young man must have stoked the stove up for her, before school. Adele stands, dropping rolled socks on the floor. She's just remembered that she needs to write the date up on the chalkboard. How could she forget? October 22, 1950, and today they're going to carve their jack-o'-lanterns, right after they take a spelling test. Harvest, cider, fathers, mothers, churn, butter, beautiful, horses.

TIP #10: Details count! Clean all the windows, in and out. Polish doorknobs. Make sure hinges do not squeak.

SO FAR, SHE'S ONLY wandered off one time. Just once, so Jack considers himself lucky, in that sense. She got almost two miles from home (he can picture how she must have looked that night, striding fast along the darkened highway in her robe and slippers, her hair blown back, eyes shining in the night). It's a miracle she wasn't killed. Now they have special locks on all the doors, and Adele wears a metal bracelet with her name and address, all the time—at least, she's supposed to. She detests the thing. Jack is always finding it in funny places, stuffed between the couch cushions or buried in the soil of potted plants.

On their most recent visit to Adele's neurologist, there was a stranger in the office, with the doctor— some intern, with a rash of pimples on his forehead. When the kid leaned forward, writing on his clipboard, the pimples shone like mountains, like the Swan range on that giant relief map in the lobby of the Forest Service headquarters. When Adele informed the intern that the current president was Richard Nixon, the corners of the young man's mouth twitched up. He glanced at the neurologist, as if Adele's wrong answer proved some fascinating point. And Jack said, "she taught Latin, did you know that? Latin."

Which she had, along with every other blessed subject, at the old two-story high school where she'd started working, once they moved to town. She was the one who had insisted that they move here, so that Jack could go to college, something he would never have imagined on his own. It was Adele who had brought home the bacon, while Jack spent his days in the high-windowed classrooms of the Forestry department, the pages of his spiral notebook riffling in the breeze of ceiling fans. She'd packed his lunch and ironed his shirts each day, while all the boys he'd grown up with, back home, were still out working in the woods, still coaxing ticks from nooks and crannies with the burning ends of cigarettes, still losing thumbs in chainsaw accidents.

Tip #11: Place fresh-cut flowers in your entryway to help potential buyers feel at home. Daffodils are always a good choice. The color yellow has been shown to trigger spending instincts in the human brain.

It's two o' clock, and Jack is busy picking out an outfit for Adele when he hears footsteps on the porch. They weren't supposed to be here yet. They weren't supposed to come till three o' clock. "Here, put this on," he says, pulling a blouse off of a hanger. "Don't leave this room. I'll be right back."

He finds Trish on the front step, fumbling with her keys. Behind her are a boy and girl who both look much too young to buy a house. The boy has facial hair; he's sporting one of those small goat-like beards that cartoon Frenchmen wear, and centaurs. Tom used to wear a beard like that in college, just to make Jack mad. The young man's face is smooth, so smooth that his small beard looks pasted-on. The girl beside him is a tiny, freckled thing, with red-gold hair and pale eyelashes. She reminds Jack of an Irish girl he used to know, before he met Adele.

"Oh," says Trish. "You're here."

"You're early," Jack says.

"No. I told you two o' clock."

"We could come back later," says the freckled girl, "If this is a bad time." She's talking in a loud, slow voice, as if she thinks Jack might be deaf, or stupid.

"No, no," Jack sighs. "Come in." He holds the door, but the girl turns and walks to the far end of the porch. She leans over the railing.

"We were just admiring your roses," she says, too loudly. "And the view. It must be really something, on a clear day."

"It is," Jack says.

"Oh yes," says Trish. "When the air's clear, you can see straight up the canyon. It's spectacular."

"What we need," says the boy, stroking his little beard. "Is wind. A good strong wind would blow this smoke right out."

Jack steps backward, almost stumbling in his haste

to get back in the house. "Please," he says, "why don't we go inside," but his voice is lost beneath the shuddering whine of another fire plane, passing overhead. They crane their necks to look at it, all four of them. "Huh," says the boy, after the plane has passed. "That was a really neat old bomber."

"A Neptune P-2V," says Jack. "To judge by the dimensions of the fuselage."

"Oh, wow," the girl says. "Wow. Are you a pilot?" She has on a sleeveless cotton dress with bra-straps peeking out from underneath. Her shoulders are as freckled as her face and her eyes, staring at Jack, are wide and green.

"No." Jack shakes his head. "I never flew planes, but I used to fight fires, once upon a time."

"Wow. That's so cool." She's talking in a normal voice, all of a sudden.

Jack opens the front door as wide as it will go. He smiles and bows, just like some television butler, ushering his guests inside with a low sweep of his arm.

Tip #12: Never let your desperation show. You won't get full market value for your house if buyers figure out you have to sell because your wife is dying a slow, agonizing death and you—poor bastard—can't keep up a place this size alone.

ADELE LOOKS OUT THE bedroom window, at the haze. The air's so thick, she can't make out the barn, the silos, or the windmill on the hill. Where is it coming from, this smoke? Is it the neighbors, burning slash again?

She'll have to ask Jack to go talk to them, when he gets home.

Tip #13: Fresh linens in the bathroom are a must. For extra zing, try fastening your towels to the rods with fabric bows in a coordinating hue.

ONCE INSIDE, JACK EXCUSES himself from his visitors and goes to check on his wife, in their room. She's as he left her, getting dressed. Jack helps her find some socks, tells her, again, that they are going to the mall. Then he remembers that she left a pile of laundry scattered in the living room, where everyone can see. "Stay here," he says. "Don't leave this room. I'll be right back."

In the living room, he gathers up the laundry, stuffs it all into the basket. As he works, he hears the clients in the kitchen, talking. They don't know that Jack is there.

"It looks so dated." That's the young man talking. "Look at that linoleum. My God! That fridge."

"It takes a special kind of person," Trish is saying. "One with vision, one who can see past certain minor flaws and understand the equity potential here. You have to think location, and square footage."

"Oh, yes." The pretty girl's voice. "Yes, this place is big, for what they're asking. Plus, I've always wanted to live someplace with a view."

Jack stuffs two more towels in the basket and starts heading down the hall. Too late, the guests are there already. "It's an ideal floor plan," Trish is saying, "lots of room to start a family someday. Spacious living room.

Three bedrooms up and laundry on the . . ." She stops. Her clients stop, too. Adele is in the way.

Jack drops the laundry basket and starts jogging down the hall. "Well, you must be Jack's wife," he hears the agent saying. "It's so nice to meet you, at long last." Adele stares at Trish's outstretched hand, but doesn't touch it. Adele is fully dressed, Jack is relieved to see, with all the buttons done up on her blouse.

"Sweetheart," Jack says, out of breath. "Let's go and find your shoes. We're going to take a little drive." He takes her arm, but Adele doesn't budge. She's staring at the clients.

"You really think that you can get away with this?" she says.

The girl's mouth opens, wordlessly. The boy moves closer to her, putting a protective arm around her shoulders. "Oh, ma'am," says Trish, "I'm sorry if we came at a bad time."

"You two just think that you can do whatever you please? Is that it?"

Jack sees the girl take the boy's hand, prepared for flight. Trish looks at Jack, her raised, plucked eyebrows seeking explanation. He has not told her about his wife's condition.

"Sweetheart," Jack says, "Honey, please. These people are our guests. Let's welcome them." He tries to steer Adele back towards the bedroom, but she shakes him off.

"It's a school night," says Adele. Her cheeks are flushed. "You have a curfew for a reason. Do you hear me? Why are you just standing there ? Have you gone deaf?"

It's more than Jack can bear, the way the freckled girl is looking at his wife. He wants to go away, to find some small dark place and hide in there until he wastes away, but what about Adele? She's trembling. "Go on," he says to the young girl, not looking at her face. "Your mother isn't feeling well. Go on now. Please just go."

Nobody moves. The two prospective buyers (who are surely not prospective any more) just stand there, gawking, until Trish turns on them, with a stern voice. "Well, kids, what are you waiting for?" she says. "You heard your mom. You're grounded. Let's get going." And the agent shepherds them off, down the hallway, first giving the girl, who's been standing as though frozen to the spot, a gentle shove between the shoulder blades.

Jack watches as they go. Before they round the corner, Trish turns back and gives him a sad smile, and he feels a pang of something he has not felt since before the diagnosis. Jack feels as though he's found a bright green sapling, hanging on, amidst the charred ruins of a wilderness.

Tip #14: Above all, avoid sentimental thoughts about your house. Emotional attachments are a hindrance, when it comes to sales.

ADELE, RECLINING ON THE forest floor, with Jack. It's late September, 1953. Their skin is etched with patterns of crushed ferns. The members of the school board would be scandalized if they could see her now, she says. Jealous old coots, says Jack, they only wish. She laughs. He picks a dead leaf from her hair. Above, the cotton-woods shake like wet dogs and clouds, reflected in the creek, dissolve and flow. Harvest cider fathers mothers churn butter beautiful horses.

Angel of Barn Four

CALL ME THE FRIEND of underdogs and dreamers. Call me the wild-card, call me what you will. All that I have, I've built from scratch and I was proud, until I saw the brand-new trainer in Barn Four. She has an air of competence, Marlene. You can tell just by the rhythm of her boots, she is a girl who doesn't mess around.

Marlene has never seen me, but I watch her when she does her midnight checks. I hide behind the feed bins when she thinks she's all alone. She doesn't know it, but I've seen her run her fingers down a colt's bowed tendon—I have heard her muttering dark charms, her spells for victory and courage. I've watched her massage a spavined hock and I know if she would lay her hands on me, she'd fix me, too.

Call me the rescuer of hopes, the re-distributor of wealth. Please do not speak to me of fate. The average gambler thinks his luck depends on certain things: a purple rabbit's foot, the phases of the moon. The wise man knows the bookies have it rigged—they'll rob you blind, the scoundrels, like they robbed my dear old dad. That's why I'm here, to level out the field. And here's the hottest tip you'll get today: there's no such thing as luck. There's only me.

Let's say you need a certain horse to scratch before the novice handicap, you need the odds to soar or plunge. Presume you need the favorite to have an off-day, call me. I can help you. I'm a pro. Perhaps you need a briefcase full of money to change hands. No problem. Easy, peasy. I'm your man. I know which jockeys can be bought and whose head groom is on the take. I can sink a needle into the soft neck of a young thoroughbred faster than you can say "amphetamine" and I won't leave a mark, I never do.

My job demands a low profile: a shame, since I take pains to look my best. I keep my hair neat, parted on one side. I shine my shoes. I wear a suit. Strange to admit, I never realized that I was lonely, until now. I have a great respect for whores, my fellow creatures of the night. I was content, until the day I saw her striding down the barn aisle, with her dog. Marlene was twirling a red leadrope, like a lariat. Her terrier was struggling to keep up.

She was wearing the same hat she always wears. A brown felt cavalryman's hat, pulled low. Her hair in a single braid. No makeup. Marlene has no use for artifice. She isn't like the others, I can tell.

I can't reveal my tricks, but I'll say this: a turkey baster full of chicken blood is the best way to fake a nosebleed in a horse. Marlene doesn't know it, but that's why her Northern Dancer filly failed the vet check right before her maiden race, three weeks ago. This was the day before I first set eyes on Marlene in her felt hat, back before I was in love.

True fact: corruption has a scent. I'd know it anywhere: the sticky-sweet of wanting more, the musky odor of entitlement. My true love smells like second-cut alfalfa and Absorbine liniment and Fiebing's saddle soap. As I explained, she doesn't mess around. I've known this since the day I saw her burst into the tackroom, where a junior groom was finishing his cigarette. Smoking is not allowed in any barn where there are beasts who lack the sense to flee from fire, but help is hard to find these days, so many trainers look the other way when grooms light up. Not Marlene. Not my pearl. She started beating the poor groom about the head with her red rope, then chased him all the way outside, into the dark. I'd never thought about a different life, before that night.

TOMORROW IS A RACE day, and sometime before the dawn, I need to do a job for an old pal, for old times' sake. I need to treat a stakes horse in Barn Nine. I have the syringe in my pocket, now, full of a fluid extracted from the skin of jungle frogs. The stuff works wonders but the side effects can be unfortunate. My old pal's not the sentimental sort.

It's almost daybreak. In an hour, this silence will be gone: the Northern Dancer filly will start banging on her door, demanding grain. The exercise boys will trade drinking stories as they lace their paddock boots. Marlene will be outside, already, sipping coffee while she watches some horse trot in a small circle, making sure he's sound enough to run.

I should be taking care of business in Barn Nine, yet here I lurk, behind the feed bins in Barn Four. My heart is pounding like a colt's—a colt with magic frog-juice in his veins. I've come to a decision and I can't turn back, old pal be damned. I want Marlene to see my face.

No doubt, she's heard my name—how could she not? I will assure her that the legends all are true, but that I'm ready for a change. We will leave this place forever, she and I. We'll buy a little stud farm in the Adirondacks, or someplace out west. I have the funds. Aside from female consorts and new suits, I don't spend much. I have enough to get a place, some sweet two-story farmhouse with a covered porch and a small pond out back. We'll get ourselves a metal driftboat. We will drift.

On our farm, all the horses' papers will be genuine, and match the tattooed numbers on their lips. We'll give no medicines that aren't prescribed. And if, per-chance, one of my old associates should find us, should come knocking with a proposition, say, a foolproof scheme involving several handicappers and a famous syndicate, I'll turn him down. I'll tell him I don't do that anymore.

She isn't here yet. While I wait, I close my eyes, imagining our pond in early morning, grey mist rising from the surface, just like steam. Is that a pebbled beach? I never learned to skip a rock. Mine was not that kind of childhood. I wonder if Marlene can show me how.

Her footsteps, finally. I wait, expecting her to walk right past my hiding spot, into the tackroom, but in-stead, she turns into the stall belonging to Sweet Balth-azar and shuts the door, leaving her terrier outside. This strikes me as a little odd. She always takes her dog into the stalls, unless the horse is dangerous, and Balthazar is gentle to a fault.

Sweet Balthazar is an enormous colt, descended from Affirmed and Secretariat, expensive, well-conformed, and still a dud. He's lackadaisical, despite his size, completely unresponsive to the whip. He's scheduled for the nine-fifteen, at forty to one odds. I could do something to improve his chances—I still have a syringe in my pocket, after all—but Marlene is not that kind of trainer. I should know.

The dog is pawing at the stall-door, whining. Pitiful. I pick him up and set him to one side, then slide the door back on its rollers, without sound. I step inside. She doesn't see me. She is crouched beside the colt's right foreleg with a small brush and a silver can. At first, I think it's hoof dressing—my true love makes her own from pine tar, neatsfoot oil and turpentine—but then I catch a whiff and I can scarce believe my nostrils. It is paint.

I've done some color jobs, myself, and I could tell Marlene that Lady Clairol is a better choice, that spray paint has a tendency to run. But right now I'm busy trying to make sense of what I'm seeing: my Marlene, the last honest trainer, and this horse who looks exactly like the long-shot Balthazar, except for that white sock on his right foreleg. Sweet Balthazar has no white markings. Hence the paint.

"Marlene." It's difficult to breathe. "My God, Marlene. You're going to pull a swap."

A ring-in is a thing of beauty, there's no doubt. It's

risky, though. Fine Cotton, Royal School, and Flockton Grey—all legendary swaps, and all got caught. A ring-in's not a job for rookies. Everyone knows that.

Marlene is staring, wild-eyed as this horse, who lacks Sweet Balthazar's calm temperament, it seems. At this moment, I can't say which pains me more: the revelation that my true love is dishonest or the fact that there's chicanery afoot on my home turf, and nobody called me.

"Who," she says finally, "are you?"

I reach my hand out. "I'm your man."

The pitchfork seems to come from nowhere, hurtling towards my head. I duck and let the steel tines hit the wall, then twist the handle out of Marlene's grasp. I fling the implement into the barn aisle, where it clangs and clatters, frightening the dog. "Marlene," I say. She's cowering against the wall. "Oh, Marlene. Why?"

I take a step in her direction and the horse wheels his hindquarters toward me, pinning back his ears. "Whoa. Easy, champ." I edge around him, touch his shoulderblade. "Be calm." I move my hand in circles, very slowly, like a mare licking her newborn foal, and before long, the big horse drops his head.

"What do you want?" whispers Marlene. Thin bars of moonlight from the window stripe her face. She has a tiny scar beside her mouth. I'm so close I could touch her, now. I don't.

The colt who isn't Balthazar is dozing, while I trace slow circles on his neck. I close my eyes and see the stud-farm, barn and trees, the cool black surface of our pond. I cannot see our driftboat, but I feel the silent pull of oars. No fish, but I can see concentric rings expanding on the water and I hear Marlene's breathing—shallow, fast—this cannot be the rugged angel of Barn Four. This girl is an imposter, like her horse.

"What do you want?" she says. I open my eyes wide. "Tell me, Mister. You can have it. Anything, okay?" I can't believe this. She must think I'm going to turn her in to the authorities, get her warned off the track for life. Clearly, she still has no idea who I am.

"Anything," she says again. I tilt my head.

The pond is gone now, vanished in the mist. My brain is full of new imaginings, instead. Marlene may be a cheater but she's still a woman. I am still a man.

Excessive loneliness can kill you, I have heard. It causes indigestion, makes your food taste bland. Habitual solitude can trigger joint pain and insomnia and judgment errors. It can make a person lose sight of his principles. Almost.

"Marlene." I shake my head, full of regret. Call me a wild-card, sure, but I am not that kind of man.

BACK IN MY SMALL motel room, taking stock. Here is my towel, hung neatly on the rack. Here is my razor, used just hours ago, when I still believed that love was possible for me. The Gideon Bible and a racing program on the nightstand, where I keep my reading glasses, too. Half a carton of Chinese food on the table and, above this, on the wall, a painting of a beach with palm trees and a happy couple strolling, hand in hand. Alone I've always been. Alone, alone.

I stretch myself diagonally across the bed, where I've arranged the bills in tidy rows, all those identical Ben Franklins smirking up. The paper crackles under me as I roll side to side, remembering how her fingers brushed my palm as we completed our transaction, recalling how our voices mingled as we counted, higher, higher, how we reached the sum at the same moment, just as the first pale rays of sunlight hit the barn. Alone. I gather up an armful of the cash and plunge my face into it, sniffling, moaning, imagining plump round numbers and her skin.

Vaquero

SIX MONTHS AFTER MY husband's stroke, I met the shepherd. I don't mean that in the figurative sense—I'm not that type. I mean an actual shepherd, one who tends the sheep which graze the rugged mountainside above our house.

The shepherd is from Mexico, from Veracruz. The dialect there differs from the one in Zacatecas, where I spent my Peace Corps years, and also from the one in Merida, where, long ago, I honeymooned with Thom.

I met my shepherd on a Wednesday, early June, while I was on my morning hike. The bitterroot and lupine were in bloom. Matisse, my dachshund, was off-leash and chasing squirrels. When I reached the south slope, where the forest ends and there are only a few Ponderosa, twisted into odd shapes by the wind, I stopped. I've always loved that view: the valley floor, our house, the college campus, the whole town. All this, and not a hundred yards away, a sight I'd never seen in all my years of following that trail.

It was an honest-to-God covered wagon, painted green. The type you sometimes see in front of roadside pioneer museums, except that this one was in good repair. The canvas top looked new. I'd barely started to consider explanations—if some fool was going to stage a wild west reenactment on my precious mountain, there'd be hell to pay—when my dog yelped and a pair of border collies pinned him down.

"Get off! Get out of here, you beasts!" I whacked at the assailants with my staff. The collies paid no notice. They were rolling Matisse back and forth between them, on the ground. I seized the nearest fluffy tail and the dog connected to it spun around and pulled me off my feet and then broke free. My dog escaped and started running back the way we'd come, the border collies nipping at his heels.

And then, the voice. A deep voice, saying "stop" in Spanish, and the collies both abandoned chase and slunk away into the trees. I was still sitting where I'd fallen, on the trail. A shadow lengthened over me and I looked up, shading my eyes, and saw a stranger on a horse. A man in a sombrero on a horse the color of dense fog and yes, it did occur to me that I had suffered some sort of cerebral accident, like Thom's. I touched my head to see if it was still intact, while the stranger stepped down from his saddle, asking in Spanish, was I hurt?

In different circumstances, I would certainly have chastised him for his aggressive dogs. I might even have threatened legal action, but as it turned out, I could not speak at all, too startled by the silver conchas on the stranger's hatband, by his open-necked white shirt, his thin mustache. He helped me stand and only then did I notice the sheep, fanned out across the meadow, and remember something I'd seen on the news, the week before. The city had used tax money to buy one-hundred-twenty head of sheep as an experiment in weed control.

The shepherd's name is Javier and he is unhappy in this country. He speaks little English and has no affinity for sheep. These facts, and others, I learned shortly after I revealed that I could speak his language. Javier is not a shepherd normally—he wanted me to know this right away. Javier is a vaquero. He took this Northern Rockies job because he saw an advertisement on the internet. Alas, the ad had been misleading; he'd believed that he'd be herding cattle, here.

I wasn't sure if he was being serious. I was fairly certain that the true vaqueros had been gone a century, or more. I thought, perhaps, this man was having fun at the expense of an old, gray-haired Gringa, which is how I must have looked to him.

"*¿El vaquero?*" He could not have missed the skepticism in my voice. "*¿El internet?*"

"*Sí.* Craigslist," Javier showed no sign of mirth. "*Un advertisement por vaquero.*" He'd been duped, not that he was complaining. No, the city council paid him well; they'd procured his visa and the covered wagon and a rented portapotty—he was trying to make the best of things. Still, he hated sheep. Sheep were stupid, said Javier, and I asked him, stupider than cows? He grinned. Cattle were "*muy estupidos,*" he admitted. But sheep! He made his thumb and forefinger into the shape of an imaginary gun and shot himself.

SINCE MY RETIREMENT, I have grown more serious about my hiking. Thomas used to hike with me, before his stroke. After the C.V.A.—to borrow the official jargon—

my husband more or less quit going out and often, when I try to leave, he clings to me. Some days, I have to pry his fingers from my arm, one at a time.

C.V.A.: that's what the doctors say these days, instead of "stroke." Cerebrovascular Accident—a term which always makes me want to punch someone. Accident, they say, as if this thing that happened to my husband is equivalent to tripping over untied laces, spilling wine. Oops, there goes his anterior communicating artery, his understanding of what's real and not. Oh dear, there goes his whole distinguished scholarly career, his eleven books, his national endowments. Oopsy-dee.

"You're lucky, Astrid." His nurse actually said this. "Your husband can still walk and talk. It could have been much worse, I hope you know."

Confabulation is a rare but famous symptom of a lesion in the anterior hypothalamus, the cingulate gyrus or the basal forebrain. Thom confabulates, which is a euphemistic way of saying he tells lies. And not just small ones—whoppers, too. For instance, he tells people we have kids and grandkids, which we don't. He claims to play the saxophone. He can't. He spins elaborate yarns about his past careers, apocryphal. His doctors told me that these symptoms might diminish over time but if anything, they have intensified. A few days after I met Javier, Thom told our brand-new neighbors, Duke and Lucy Tubbs, that he was once the cook aboard a naval submarine.

"How fascinating," Lucy said.

"Which war?" asked Duke. The Tubbs moved here

from Omaha, Nebraska. They had stopped by to introduce themselves, but I was not at home. I was out hiking with the dog, so Thom answered the door.

"Korean," Thomas said. The thing is, he looks normal, to the untrained eye. His smile is slightly asymmetrical, these days, but unless you know him like I do, you probably wouldn't notice.

"Ah," Duke nodded. "I had an uncle in Korea. Uncle Pete."

"Sure, I remember him," my husband said. "That shifty-looking bugger with the glass eye." Then he shut the door. I found out about this several days after it happened, when I met Lucy for the first time, on the loop trail. She told me what Thom said and I had to make the usual apologies, explain that he was never in the military, that we're pacifists, that Thomas wrote some well-regarded books about the uses of non-violence in labor movements all around the world.

"He doesn't know he's lying," I told Lucy. "To him, I guess, the memories are real."

"That must be very hard." She'd fallen into step beside me on the trail, our footfalls cushioned by the layers of forest detritus, the dappled sunlight softening her face. Lucy is probably my age. It's hard to tell, though, since she dyes her hair. She's cute and dainty, not at all like me. I'm sure she was the kind of girl who twirled batons in high school, while I was reading Kierkegaard and wearing Che Guevara boots, size twelve. I've never been petite. In high school, I was always hungry, too afraid to eat lest I gain weight. I wasn't trying to impress the boys—I knew I was invisible to them. My motivations were political; I loathed the thought of getting fat while people elsewhere in the world were dying of starvation, every day.

Lucy has probably never had to watch her figure, but here's an interesting truth: on that steep, uphill trail, she proved to be less fit than she appears. In fact, she struggled to keep up with me.

"You know," said Lucy, as she mopped her sweaty forehead with her sleeve. "I used to take care of my dad, in his last years. He lived with us. So if you ever need someone to stay with Thomas…"

"Look," I said. "A mountain bluebird. See it?"

"Where?" Lucy squinted. "Anyway, if you need someone to stay with Thomas for a while, so you can get out of the house…"

"I am out. What do you call this?" I waved my staff at the surrounding trees. "And Thomas doesn't need a babysitter, thank you. We're just fine." I could tell I'd hurt her feelings, but I hadn't even said the things I'd wanted to. I never said, for instance, that my husband might be fourteen years my senior but he's still a good man, kind and gentle and still very well-regarded in his field. I didn't tell her that my Thom is still a far cry from her doddering old dad.

Lucy was silent until after we had reached the second switchback. Then she asked me if I'd met the shepherd yet.

"Javier, you mean?" I was surprised, I must admit. She'd hardly been in town a week and already she'd grown cozy with the shepherd, *el vaquero*?

"Isn't he wonderful?" she said. "When I first saw him in that hat…oh, my!" She fanned herself.

"Well, that sombrero has a practical purpose, you know. Where he's from, the sun shines about three hundred days a year. He doesn't wear it to impress old ladies, like ourselves."

She stammered, "Oh, no, no, I only meant…" Her voice trailed off and pretty soon, all I could hear was Lucy's labored breathing—I'd picked up the pace. We didn't talk for the remainder of the hike and we did not see Javier, much to Lucy's disappointment, I am sure. He must have taken his flock elsewhere for the day.

Later on, I wondered if I'd been too harsh. I believe in honesty; I subscribe to a policy of truth, but sometimes truth can be a bitter pill, I know. I felt a little guilty. Still, in Lucy's case, I decided it was for the best. I had no time for busybodies, anyway.

Yet, two days later, she was knocking at our door. "I'm going to take this quiche up to the shepherd," she said. "Want to come along?"

"You're taking him a quiche?" Was this what people did, I asked myself, in Omaha?

"It's kale and Gruyere. It's my daughter's recipe," she said. "We have a ton of kale, now, in our garden. If you guys want some, ever, say the word."

It took us almost a half hour to get to reach the meadow—though it was just a mile or two, uphill. Lucy hiked slowly to preserve the quiche, or so she claimed. As we neared the forest's edge, she stopped and fished a Spanish dictionary from her pack. "Wait here. I'll go ahead and tell the shepherd that we're coming so he can call his dogs off. Let me see," she started flipping through the book. "Dogs. Dammit. How do you say 'dogs'?"

"'*Los perros.*' Here." I handed her the leash. "You wait here with Matisse. I'll talk to Javier."

"Oh, sure, fine. Hey, you'll need this." She handed me her dictionary. I gave it back to her.

"Wow. You speak Spanish? Really?" She looked so impressed that, for a moment, I felt sad for her.

Javier greeted me with arms held wide. I've never been a hugger, so I veered away to pet his dogs. We chatted while I helped him chain the collies and before long, I forgot all about my neighbor. I was actually surprised when I looked up and saw her side-stepping down the steep trail, my dog's leash in one hand and her quiche balanced on the other. "*Dos Senoras!*" Javier said. I couldn't tell if he was pleased or overwhelmed.

When Lucy reached us, Javier took the quiche and pointed at a clump of trees. "*Tengo un cordero nuevo.*" Lucy looked at me, a hint of panic on her face. Before she could get out her dictionary, I said, "He's telling you about the new lamb. Let's go look."

The lamb was less than one hour old, his fleece still damp and sticky from the amniotic fluid. Lucy was besotted. She plonked herself down in the grass, cooing and clucking, snapping countless photos of the lamb and ewe. Eventually, I had to prod her to get up, so we could get back on the trail before the sun went down.

I'm not afraid of hiking in the dark, but Thomas had been having a rough day and I needed to be home in time to make sure he took all his meds.

The whole way back, my neighbor pestered me with questions. She wanted to know the names of everything, all the local flowers and trees and animals. She asked me how I'd learned my Spanish and looked amazed when I informed her I was also fluent in three other languages. She made me tell her all about my travels. "You've led such a fascinating life," she sighed, and once again, I felt a little sad for her. Had she always lived in the Midwest? Had she been to college, traveled, dreamed about a different kind of life? I wondered these things, but I did not ask.

"This is so fun, Astrid. Isn't it? We ought to hike together every day."

"Oh, look, Camas." I knelt to inspect a purple bud. "That's the first one I've seen this year."

A little further on, she asked, "Why do the sheep wear bells?"

"So Javier can find them, when they wander off," I said, although I didn't know, in truth. I was just guessing.

"He sure likes you."

"Pshaw." And yet, the blood went to my face. Fresh air and exercise will do that, every time. "Your quiche," I said. "I'm sure he's never had a gift like that before."

"You think?" Lucy looked happy. To my surprise, I found I couldn't tell her what he'd really said. While she was busy, looking at the lamb, Javier had peeled the foil back from the Pyrex dish. He'd prodded at a kale leaf, frowning. "*¿Qué es esto?*"

THOMAS WAS UPSTAIRS IN our room when I got home from the hike. I found him sitting up in bed, reading a new book about the origins of Polish solidarity. "Any good?"

He shook his head. "The premise is outdated and the prose is lackluster, at best. How was your hike?"

"Not bad. I met one of the neighbors." I told him about Lucy while I undid the buttons on my cardigan. "Quiche, can you believe? I doubt if many people in his village have even seen a quiche. I mean, Lucy is friendly but she's clueless." I sat down on the bed to pull my socks off. "She doesn't get the socio-economic undertones. You know, the rich American bestowing gifts. Noblesse Oblige." I looked at Thomas. He'd put down his book.

"You're a sight for sore eyes," Thomas said. "You remind me of my favorite Delacroix. You know the one."

"Liberty Leading the People?"

"Bingo."

I was happy. He hadn't talked that way in a long time. I pulled the bedspread back, thinking that possibly that nurse was right. Maybe I should be grateful that my husband was still physically intact.

He said he loved me and I kissed his cheek. "I never will forget the way I felt when I first saw you," he said. "The way you looked, up on that stage."

"What stage?"

"You could have had your pick of any man."

I bit my lower lip. "Please, Thomas. Don't." Even though the doctors tell me that my husband's symptoms are involuntary, out of his control, I can't help feeling, often, that he must be doing this on purpose, that he's making fun of me.

"That very first time I saw you dance, I knew I had to make you mine."

"Thom, stop. You know I've never danced a step in my whole life."

"Such modesty. You were the star of that revue."

"Oh, quit it. Quit this, now." Sometimes I have this fantasy that Thomas is just playing an elaborate joke, that one day soon he'll snap back to his old self, saying "fooled you!" and I won't be angry, even, just relieved. I closed my eyes and said, in what I hoped was a calm tone, "we met when I was in my Master's program, back East. You were my graduate advisor. It would have been a scandal, if it hadn't been the sixties."

He looked at me, his head tipped to one side. "Sure, I know that," he said. "You were my smartest student," and I could have wept, right then, from gratitude.

"Yes, yes," I whispered. "That was me."

"And after school, at night, you danced. You had that costume with the feathers."

"Oh, for Christ's sake, Thomas. I did not!"

He flinched. He doesn't like it when I yell. I climbed out of bed and put my bathrobe on and tied the belt in a square knot. I'm not supposed to argue with him when he starts confabulating. I know that.

His neurologist suggests that I should try to steer the conversation in a new direction, whenever Thom's false stories get too wild. "Try another topic, see if you can find some neutral ground. Above all, don't lose patience. Remind yourself that this is not his fault." Fair enough, but lately I have found that I can tell myself all sorts of useful things. Believing them —ah, therein lies the rub.

"So anyway," I said, after a few deep breaths. "I was telling you about our neighbor. She's absurd. She acts as if she's got some kind of a crush on Javier, even though he must be in his forties. Young enough to be her son." I went over to the dresser and picked up my hairbrush, pulled some hairs out of the bristles. "It would be amusing if it weren't so condescending. I mean, it's just another form of ethnic stereotyping, isn't it? The romanticized interpretation of the foreigner. The sexual objectification of the Latin male."

"Javier? Javier who?"

"Remember, Thomas, I was telling you about the shepherd that the city hired to..."

"Shepherd?" he said, clearly peeved. "There aren't any shepherds nowadays. Quit talking gibberish and let me sleep."

THE DAY AFTER THE stroke, one of the nurses asked if there was anyone I wanted her to call.

"Not really."

"No friends? Relatives?" she said.

"Look, if I want to call someone, I'll call them. Understand?" I hated how the nurse looked at me then, her eyes so full of pity. We had friends. Thomas and I were held in high regard by all our colleagues, several of whom called, eventually, to ask how he was doing. We had a very decent social life before the stroke and we could have had one after, if we'd wanted. Our priorities had changed. Thomas tired so quickly and I had to keep on track with all his meds. Also, I had my garden—that took up a lot of time.

Besides, and this is something I could never tell that nurse, I can't let our former colleagues see my Thomas in his present state. He is a famous scholar, after all. I can just picture Adrian LaRue, that lazy sycophant they hired last year, spreading gossip in the history department office. "Poor bastard's lost his marbles," Adrian will snicker, as he entertains our former colleagues with ridiculous untruths he's heard from Thom. Well, he can go to hell—I won't let Adrian or anybody else rob Thomas of his dignity. I know my Thom would do the same for me.

LUCY JOINED ME ON my hikes for the remainder of the week. And then, on Saturday, I rose at a full hour earlier than usual, at five o'clock. I'd noticed that the lights did not go on next door until six-thirty, at the earliest. I laced my boots while Thomas snored. I left Matisse at home.

The sun was just cresting the ridgeline when I reached Javier's wagon. He was sitting on a milk-crate, oiling tack. He stretched a latigo across his knees and I noticed the tattoo on his left forearm. Two letters with a bar beneath, identical to the brand on his horse's flank. If this man was not a real vaquero, I decided then, he must be something close. He asked me where my friend was and at first, I thought he meant Matisse. Then I realized that he was asking about Lucy.

"No, no." I shook my head. "*Lucy no es mi amiga.*"

Already, at that hour, he was dressed in his usual garb: white shirt, sombrero, chaps. His horse was grazing, hobbled, near the outhouse, and the border collies were curled up in the tall grass. The sheep were clustered in a trapezoidal pen, surrounded by electric wire and guarded by a dog I hadn't seen before. He was huge and black, of no determinable breed. I watched him pace, head low and hackles raised, and felt grateful that I wasn't a coyote.

I reassembled Javier's bridle while he let the sheep out of the pen. The collies woke and stretched and, as I scratched their ears, I spotted a familiar Pyrex plate under the wagon, and I smiled. The dogs had made short work of Lucy's quiche, it seemed. All that remained were slobbery bits of kale.

Many years ago, at boarding school, I studied equitation and dressage, and I still know my way around a curry comb. That morning, I helped Javier groom his mare—an Andalusian with the longest mane I'd ever seen. I picked out all her feet while Javier knelt to buckle on his spurs, then I spread the saddle blanket across her withers and swung the saddle into place, with just one hand. Javier looked up and told me I was strong.

On my way home, it seemed the forest had a pulse. I could hear the pinecones drop; I smelled the fermentation of the layers beneath my feet, releasing nitrogen into the soil. Amidst the bracken ferns and balsamroot were tiny, star-shaped flowers I could not name. I'd never noticed them before. I stepped carefully, trying not to crush the blossoms with my boots, but I couldn't help it—they were everywhere.

I started setting my alarm for five o clock each day. I left Matisse at home. Instead, I took the dog on shorter walks around the neighborhood, in early evening, when I knew the coast was clear. In this manner, I avoided Lucy for three blissful weeks, and then one morning, I slept right through the alarm. I'd been up late—Thomas had had one of his bad nights, waking often, shouting something about Russian spies. I didn't get on the trail till almost seven and—alas—there was my neighbor, crouched down in the shade, tying her shoe. "Oh, Astrid, I've been worried. Why haven't you returned my calls?"

I started to make some excuse, but Lucy interrupted me. "I got to fretting when I didn't see you on the trail. I was afraid something had happened, but then Javier told Duke that he'd seen you and everything was fine."

"Wait," I said. "Wait. Duke knows Javier?"

"Oh, sure. Duke hikes up there every afternoon. He takes a six-pack. They just sit around on camp-chairs, drinking beer."

"You're joking."

"No. Duke enjoys the company—you know how boring it can get, once you're retired. And Javier's always glad to see him. I imagine he gets lonesome, watching sheep all day."

I tried to think of something Duke might have in

common with Javier. Duke Tubbs, with his loud laugh, his massive gut, his thumbs hooked through the belt-loops of his pleated shorts—what would he have to say to a vaquero? "I didn't realize," I told her, finally, "that your husband spoke Spanish."

"Oh, he doesn't, but they get by. Sign language, and so forth. Duke says some afternoons they just sit there for a couple hours, not saying anything, just looking at the scenery, drinking their beer."

When our hike was over, Lucy asked if we would come to dinner, Sunday night. I told her that we had a prior commitment.

"Monday, then."

I shook my head. "We can't. Thom doesn't do well out of his environment." But she looked unexpectedly dis-traught—in fact, I was afraid that she might cry—and before I even knew what I was doing, I was saying, "Why don't you and Duke come over to our house, instead?"

WHICH IS HOW I FOUND myself making Thai curry for our neighbors, three days later. I'd already gotten Thom-as out of bed and made him change out of the track-suit he wore nearly every day. "You need to look respectable." I handed him a striped shirt that he used to wear on teaching days. "We're having guests."

"Guests? Who?" We hadn't had guests since—well, it had been some time.

"The Tubbs. Our neighbors," I said. "You've met them before."

"Ah, yes, the post-colonial ethnographers."

"No, I don't think so. They're from Omaha." I didn't mention that they'd owned a Chevy dealership, back home. It does no good, confusing Thomas with the facts.

My curry made the Tubbs' eyes water—I had added extra cumin—but Lucy, girl-scout that she is, pretended to enjoy it. She even asked me, dabbing at her nose, if she could have the recipe. While we ate, Thomas told our guests about our years in Prague. There were some inconsistencies in his account, but the Tubbs didn't seem to notice these. They asked a lot of questions, laughed at all his jokes. Thomas was more animated than I'd seen him in a long time and I thought that maybe this small get-together hadn't been a bad idea, after all.

"So," Duke rose to take his dishes to the sink. "Did Lucy tell you two about our latest purchase?"

"*His* purchase," Lucy clarified. "He went and bought himself an ATV, can you believe?"

I blinked.

"You know," she said. "One of those four-wheel-drive doohickeys. Like an off-road golf cart."

"Golf cart, my foot," sniffed Duke. "I'd like to see a golf cart go straight up a mountain, like this can. Rocks, stumps, you name it. It can handle anything."

I was still mystified. "But what's it for?"

"Oh," Duke said. "This and that."

"Now honey, tell the truth," said Lucy. "You bought that thing so you could haul stuff to the shepherd."

"Stuff? What kind of stuff?" I asked.

"The basics," Duke was filling up the sink. "Dogfood, paper products, toiletries."

"And beer." Lucy snapped her dishtowel at him. "Don't forget the beer."

"I still don't get it," I said. "Why's that your responsibility? Doesn't the city take care of those things?"

"Well, more or less." Duke said, scrubbing a plate. "But you should see the garbage dogfood they provide. Like processed cardboard. You can't expect a working dog to eat that crap. Hey, that reminds me. He taught me a new phrase yesterday. "*Está de la chingada.*" It means, literally, "This is shit."

Lucy took a dripping spoon out of my hand. "Men," she said. As if that explained anything at all.

They stayed till almost ten o clock. They'd brought some wine of a surprisingly good vintage and, when that was gone, we broke out the Drambuie I'd been saving since our last sabbatical. After a while, I leaned back in my chair and closed my eyes: I drifted on the flow of conversation. Lucy's excited chatter mingled with her husband's braying laugh. And Thomas, he was laughing, too—a sound I hadn't heard in a long time. Then, just when I'd decided that we should have company more often, I heard Duke's flat Midwestern drawl: "hell, I had no idea you two were mountain climbers. Wow."

I sat straight up. Across from me, Thomas was in the middle of a story, waving his arms around. "On the fourth day, Astrid slipped and fell a hundred-fifty feet into an ice crevasse." No. Not now. Just when I was beginning to enjoy myself.

"Thom," I said, and the neighbors glanced at one another, just a quick glance, but I caught it. Thomas didn't.

"So there she was,"—he waved his arms theatrically—"my wife, above the bottomless abyss..."

"Now, Thomas," I was trying to sound light-hearted. "There's no need to bore our neighbors with..."

"Are you kidding?" Duke said. "This is the best story I've ever heard."

"My strength is failing," Thomas said. "I realize I'm going to have to choose. Do I cut the rope, let my beloved fall, and spare myself? Or do I choose to perish with her?"

Thomas sipped his Scotch. I tried to smile.

"You choose to perish," Duke said, leaning forward in his chair. "Naturally, you choose to fall together."

"Bingo," Thomas set his glass down, jangling the ice. "I mean, there was never any doubt."

"Oh!" Lucy put her hand over her heart. I felt my left eye start to twitch.

"But suddenly, as luck would have it," Thom said, "I remember that I have a parachute."

I'd heard enough. "Mountain climbers do not carry parachutes," I said. "And furthermore, you're not a climber, Thomas. You're afraid of heights."

He was silent for a moment. Then he turned towards Duke. "Our sherpa gave us some advice..."

"Our sherpa?" Now my voice was shrill. "First we're alone up on some godforsaken mountain and next—abracadabra—we've got a sherpa? You're not even making sense."

"Sure he is," said Duke. "I love this story."

"No, you don't. You just feel sorry for my husband, which is not the same at all."

Nobody spoke for several seconds. Thom was staring at his drink. Then Lucy stood, clutching her purse. "It's getting late, Duke. We should go."

I STARTED HIKING TWICE a day, at dawn and dusk. I took Matisse, and kept him on the leash. I always turned back just before the meadow. I was in no mood to talk to anyone.

Sometimes, on evening hikes, I'd find a certain stump and sit there while the stars came out and bats began to swoop between the trees. I'd listen to the night sounds: owls and coyotes, and I'd contemplate the choices I have made.

I didn't have to end up here, like this. Back in the Peace Corps, there was one young man who took a shine to me—don't ask me why. When we got back to America, he was going to buy a bus and live in it. He planned to be a nomad, and start following some band I'd never even heard of. He said I ought to join him. He said everyone was doing stuff like that, back home. I did not accept the offer. I made fun of him. Chasing some long-haired rock band—how was that supposed to change the world? "It might just change your consciousness," he said. I scoffed, but I still wonder where I'd be if I'd gone down that other path. Would I be happier? Of course, if I'd done that I probably never would have earned my PhD. I never would have met my husband, written either of my books.

One night, as I was sitting on my stump, Duke Tubbs went past me, on his ATV. He stopped, a few feet down the trail and killed the engine, craned his neck around. "Astrid? Is that you?" He looked concerned. He offered me a ride, but I waved him away. He must have wondered what on earth I was doing out, alone, at that hour. Well, I could have asked the same of him.

Then came a bad day, worse than most. Thomas had grown silent, since our dinner with the Tubbs, and I'd accepted this as my just due. He barely spoke to me, he didn't read the *Times* aloud at breakfast, as has been our custom these past thirty years, and on this one bad day, he refused even to get up and dress himself. He wouldn't eat the meals I made him; once, he spat his soup out on the bedspread, claiming that I'd poisoned it. I stayed calm. I didn't shout or slam the door. When I had had enough, I went outside.

I stayed out, working in the garden, that whole afternoon and right through suppertime (let Thomas fix his own damn meals, for once). At sunset, I watched Duke's ATV come down the winding trail behind our house. I heard him shut the engine off, next door. Then I went inside, where Thomas, now, was sleeping, and I changed my clothes. I zipped a bottle of Malbec into my backpack, found a folding corkscrew and two plastic cups, and set off for the meadow, by myself.

The whole way there, I thought of things to say. "I brought this wine," I'd say, *en espagnol*, "because I thought you might be tired of quiche." He'd laugh, and there'd be nothing wrong with it. I was old enough to be his mother, for God's sake. Besides, Duke drank with

Javier every day. But why, I asked myself—if I was only being sociable—had I put on my favorite linen blouse: the one that shows the gold flecks in my eyes?

THE DOGS DIDN'T EVEN bark as I approached—they knew me well, by then. All the sheep were in their pen, already, and the Andalusian was dozing on her feet, wearing a blue mask to protect her face from flies. "Javier?" I called. The embers of a fire were smoldering between two empty camp chairs. "Javier?"

Inside the wagon, something rustled and a head poked out from underneath the canvas flap. "¿Señora?"

I had never seen Javier without his hat. He had very little hair on top. I was startled by the way his pale scalp glowed, contrasting with the warm brown of his face— so startled that, at first, I didn't notice that he had no shirt. His chest and shoulders were completely bare.

Embarrassed, I said something idiotic about unattended campfires, which was not at all what I had planned to say. I had intended to sound witty, erudite, and there I was: impersonating Smokey Bear. No matter, though, because just then, a second face appeared beneath the flap. And she wasn't wearing a shirt either, it appeared.

The shepherd introduced us. "Astrid...Carmela." Carmela, it turned out, was Javier's girlfriend, visiting from Mexico. He'd never mentioned her to me, but then, why would he?

Carmela smiled. She was thirty-ish, with a cleft chin and almond eyes. I couldn't see much of her, just enough to tell that she was waif-like, delicate, the perfect opposite of me.

"*Lo siento*," I said. "Sorry, sorry..." Backing up, I tripped on Javier's boots, which were lying in the grass. I fell, jumped up and hurried off in the direction I had come, the corkscrew in my backpack clanking rhythmically against the still unopened bottle.

Javier called after me, but I was gone. I'd left my body. I could see myself as they must see me, as a strange old woman like the ones who menace princesses in fairy tales. A huge crone lumbering down mountains, waking sheep and lovers, tremoring the earth with my giant feet.

THE VERY NEXT DAY, when I thought that things could not get any worse, my husband tumbled down a hill and broke his leg. He left the house while I was at the grocery store. He tried to take Matisse out for a walk—I don't know what possessed him—and he slipped. Lucy was the one who found him, after she looked out her kitchen window and saw our dog trot past, dragging his leash.

Thom spent four days and three nights in the hospital. I stayed there with him, sleeping for short stretches on a vinyl sofa in the waiting room. Lucy stayed, too, although I told her to go home. Duke came and went, bringing us takeout from the Chinese restaurant. "Oriental food," he called it, and I was too exhausted to correct him. On the third night, he brought along a guest.

The nurse's aide was in our room when Javier entered, his spurs clanking with each step. When she saw him in his hat and chaps, she nearly dropped the bed-pan she was holding. Javier sat down beside my husband's bed. He doffed his hat and crossed himself. Beneath the harsh fluorescent light, he looked even balder than I had remembered. What hair he had was plastered to his head in a low circle, like a bathtub ring. Also, he had a small pot-belly. I had never noticed this before. Too much of Duke's cerveza, I supposed. He glanced at me. "*¿Cómo está?*"

I shrugged. I gestured at my sleeping Thomas, at the IV in his arm, the beeping monitor beside his bed. "*Está de la chingada,*" I said. This is shit.

We ate fried rice and fortune cookies. I inquired about Carmela and learned she'd gone back to Veracruz. Her visa had expired. Javier heaved a sigh and I recognized the sound of loneliness. I could write the book on loneliness, I thought.

After an hour or so, Thom woke. He rolled to his left side and looked at Javier, then rolled back to his right and looked at me. "Who's that?"

"I am the shepherd," Javier said, in English.

Thomas closed his eyes.

THE NEXT THREE WEEKS, I didn't set foot on the trail. I took Matisse on very short walks around the block. Thomas didn't leave his bed. When I had to go somewhere, I blocked the staircase with a heavy piece of furniture, to keep him safe.

The dog grew whiny and the phone and doorbell rang throughout the day. I didn't answer. Mornings, when I stepped outside to get the paper, I found casseroles wrapped in tin foil on our porch and once, a Tupperware container full of pasta salad, garnished with fresh kale.

One evening, working in my garden, I looked up and saw the sheep strung out along the trail, up on the mountain. I heard the far-off tinkling of their bells, like windchimes, and I wished that I could be different sort of person than I am. I have missed out on certain things, I know. I've been too quick to judge, too proud. Quite possibly, I have not loved the human race enough, though I have tried. But at my age one understands that there's a time when change is possible and later on, a time when it's too late.

When I went in to check on Thomas, he was already asleep. I started drawing all the blinds. There was some damage to one window screen, I saw. The dog had clawed it loose, along the bottom edge. My little dog was going crazy, cooped up in the house. My poor Matisse. And then I noticed that the upper border of the screen was damaged, too, and the top edge was six feet from the floor. It was not the dog who had been clawing to get out.

THE NEXT DAY, EARLY, I picked up the phone and dialed. Lucy answered on the second ring.

IT TOOK US ALL DAY to get ready for the trip. Duke built a plywood platform on his cargo trailer, and we fastened a chaise lounge on top, so Thom could keep his leg extended comfortably. We attached the crutches to the ATV with bungee cords and strapped the cooler underneath. When we finally embarked, that evening, Duke drove slowly, inching up the trail. Lucy and I walked alongside the trailer, one on each side, holding Thom's hands and keeping him in place.

By the time we got there, it was almost dark. "He'll have to walk the last bit," Duke said, shutting off the engine. "I don't want to spook the horse."

The three of us helped Thom negotiate the bumpy ground. I was nervous, shouting warnings about rocks and gopher holes, but Thom did fine. Javier, meanwhile, was busy rounding up the sheep and herding them into their pen. We set Thom's chaise lounge up beside the fire and Lucy tucked an afghan around his legs.

When Javier returned, Duke handed him a beer while Thomas stared.

"You really are a shepherd," Thomas said.

"No," Javier gave a melancholy smile. "*Soy un vaquero.*"

We sat around the fire and watched the stars come out while Lucy practiced phrases from her Spanish dictionary. "*Muy bueno,*" Javier told her. Then he asked me, didn't I think Lucy had been making splendid progress?

"*Sí.*" It turns out Thom is not the only person who can fib.

And later, after the coyotes started yipping, not far off, and the big black guard dog paced outside the pen, Thomas told us a long story which bore minimal resemblance to objective truth, assuming such a truth exists—I cannot say for certain anymore. The sheep made

soft sounds and the moon appeared and disappeared behind the clouds and we listened to the cadence of Thom's
words, the rise and fall. In his voice there is a landscape,
covered with our tracks. And unmapped regions, lakes
and deserts, places we have never been, except in dreams.

Covenants

1. ORANGE DOOR.

It wasn't always like this. At the start, we liked them very much; we all believed that it would do us good to have a younger family around. Our own offspring, you understand, are fully grown; this neighborhood was quiet before the Morrows moved into the neo-Tudor on the cul-de-sac, bringing their Isabella, five months old. A precious thing. Mrs. Maxwell loved the baby's dimples and Mrs. Jepson gushed about her curls, though even then, we sensed that there was something not entirely right about the child. When we stopped by the Morrows' house, en masse, bearing our gifts—the ficus tree, the crocheted boots, the platinum plate engraved with Isabella's name—the baby girl looked through us, as if we were ghosts.

2. ORANGE PIGGY BANK.

Of course, most neighborhoods have covenants, but oftentimes, the rules are not enforced. In our community, all new homeowners are invited to a two-hour presentation by the neighborhood association, to familiarize them with the codes and by-laws that protect our equity, our way of life. It's important that newcomers know the covenants, because the penalties for violations are severe. The fines start at five hundred dollars, for a first infraction, and we have a three-strikes clause included in our ordinances, allowing us to force repeat offenders out. We don't have to use it often. We're thankful for that.

No one anticipated any problems with the Morrows. They were so quiet and tidy—he was conscientious with the yard and she was tasteful, always, in her choice of holiday décor. And when we waited seven weeks for cards to thank us for those welcome gifts, we let it go. Well, all of us except for Mrs. Troy, who said she was surprised, she'd thought that Mrs. Morrow had more class than that. But Mrs. Betts reminded her that Mrs. Morrow worked outside the home.

3. ORANGE BLANKET.

In their garage, they kept a new white crib, in parts. We spied it there one Saturday when we were on our morning stroll and he was in his driveway, detailing his car. Mrs. Taylor asked him, "Doesn't Isabella need that crib?" and he told us that his daughter couldn't stand confinement—she screamed bloody murder in her carseat, loathed her stroller. "We can't even get her near a playpen," he confessed, then told us that the baby slept between him and his wife, all three of them together on their king-sized bed. Poor Mrs. Taylor flushed, when he said that. We gave her a hard time about it, later. Mrs. Troy said, "Don't you wish you hadn't asked?"

4. ORANGE CURTAIN.

Two years went by. He kept the hedges neatly pruned in summer and in winter, always had the sidewalks cleared of snow before our morning walks. If only everyone were so considerate. The inside of the house was clean, as well, on those increasingly rare days when she invited us inside, though we noted that the windows needed work. The glass was smudged with tiny hand and nose prints, constantly. Clean windows are, of course, mandated by our covenants, but we were kind. We're mothers, all. We understand that children take a toll.

One morning, just a few months after her fourth birthday, Isabella snuck out of the house before her parents were awake. The Morrows were beside themselves, of course—they thought that she'd been kidnapped. There were four police cars in the cul-de-sac by eight A.M. But the child had not been snatched, as it turned out. She'd gone no further than the Morrow's own front yard, where she'd climbed up a tree. She was perched there the whole time, on a branch twelve feet above the ground, while we swarmed through the cul-de-sac, calling her name. She sat there, watching, while we crawled on hands and knees through spiky clumps of potentilla, she sucked her thumb while we ransacked the Carters' garden shed. "Imagine," Mrs. Betts said, afterwards. "Just four years old and that far up a tree!" It took two men to get the little girl back down.

5. ORANGE GEM.

After their second nanny quit, a grandmother arrived to stay with them. Mr. Morrow's mother, Gwen. A jewel, she was. Over the span of countless conversations by the mailbox, Gwen verified what we had surmised, on own own: wee Isabella had become unmanageable. We knew that she had tantrums. We had heard her wailing, sometimes, as we passed the house—a high-pitched sound that made our small dogs nervous. But we'd had no idea that these fits could last for two hours or more, and could be triggered by the most inconsequential things, such as her grandmother's attempts to cut her nails ("You ought to see them—they're just claws"), to make her try just one bite of her dinner, or wear a periwinkle sailor suit that Gwen had bought for her at Nordstrom's end-of-season sale. "The only color Isabella wears is orange," Gwen told us, and we shook our heads. Mrs. Jepsen said it went to show the dangers of permissive parenting.

A shame, since Isabella was apparently advanced, in other ways. At eighteen months, she had been reading cereal box labels and now, at four, she understood subtraction and could name the U.S. presidents, in order. But that temper. The child, upset because she couldn't wear her favorite orange pajamas for the fourth night in a row, had bitten Gwen. We saw the marks. Poor Gwen had raised four children, none of which had ever bitten her or her late husband—at least, never hard enough to break the skin.

6. ORANGE EGG.

At Easter, Isabella climbed another tree, and jumped from there onto the gabled roof next door, earning a brief spot on the evening news and visit from the Child and Family Services department.

7. ORANGE PLANE.

There was a name for it, what Isabella had. After the roof-top escapade, the Morrows took her to some specialists, but no one told us what the verdict was. "I don't care what those so-called experts call it," Gwen said. This was right before she flew back home to Minneapolis. "I don't care what they tell me. Spoiled is spoiled."

A jewel, Gwen was, but still, one wondered why she didn't recognize that there was something genuinely wrong. The child was lovely, huge grey eyes and Shirley Temple hair, but it was difficult to see her face because she kept the collars of her orange shirts pulled up high around her face. She never answered when we spoke to her and she liked to make her two hands act as puppets and have conversations with them, which sounds sweet, but wasn't, really. From time to time, outside the grocery store, leaving the mall, we'd see small Isabella raging, writhing on the sidewalk in a red-faced, screaming fit. It made us think about how fortunate we were.

And yet, after the diagnosis, things got better for a while. There were no more escape attempts, thanks to a set of child-proof door and window locks installed by

Mr. Morrow. And a schoolbus started coming to the cul-de-sac each day, to ferry Isabella to a special preschool in the city.

8. ORANGE BUS.

When we were children, was there such a thing as special education? We didn't know. Mrs. Maxwell said she thought people with physical deformities were kept behind closed doors, back then, and Mrs. Troy agreed. Were we to blame if we were caught off-guard by that poor, moon-faced boy who rode on Isabella's bus? We did our best. When he raised his shriveled arm to greet us, we waved back.

To say nothing of the young man with the pockets — little Aidan. We learned his name because the Morrows threw a party and invited all of Isabella's preschool classmates to their home. Wee Aidan spent the whole time near the sandbox, with his two hands tucked inside his underwear, and his mother—a big woman in a flowered dress—kept calling, from across the lawn: "Aidan! Hands in pockets! Hands in pockets, son!" We all love children, here, but it was generally agreed that this was not the sort of thing one's guests should have to witness from one's patio, while waiting for their hamburgers to brown.

Still, Isabella seemed to be improving. We saw her, with increasing frequency, out running errands with her mother, playing at the park. Sometimes the two of them held hands, which was a thing the child had not allowed before. Isabella still refused to speak to us, but we noticed that the tantrums had begun to taper off. She had a little book she carried with her, all the time, inside a see-through plastic purse. She called the thing "my calm-down book" and every page had a picture of some orange thing pasted to it. Half were crayon pictures she had made herself; the rest had been clipped out of magazines.

Whenever Isabella started getting antsy, jaw clenched, tiny hands balled into fists, her mother helped her take the book out of her purse. "Orange shoes," she'd say, and turn the page. "Orange socks." Soon Isabella would join in. "Orange elephant," they'd say together. "Orange snake. Orange giraffe." As they flipped through the homemade book, the child's fingers would uncurl, one at a time. Her breathing slowed, her voice came down in pitch. "Orange sun." It sounded like a chant. "Orange cloud. Orange moon. Orange stars."

9. ORANGE TRUCK.

Most times, we know when someone's marriage is in trouble. Most often, there are signs: a basement light left on all night, the sound of slamming doors. We weren't surprised when the McHughs split up, right in the middle of a sixty-thousand-dollar kitchen renovation. Mrs. Moore, who lives next door to the McHughs, had seen an unfamiliar car parked in their driveway Sunday afternoons, while Ben McHugh was at the racquet club. But in the Morrows' case, we had no clue. We all thought everything was fine until the moving van showed up, that March, to take his things away.

Mrs. Morrow got the house, and Isabella.

10. Orange umbrella.

After Mr. Morrow left, it rained for three straight weeks. Our lawns filled in. A plastic grocery bag, blown by the wind, snagged in the upper branches of our neighbor's tree, and there it stayed. We worried that she was not coping well. We all felt something should be done, but what? We talked about it at the gym, the clubhouse, at the next association meeting. We couldn't very well send flowers; nobody had died. A card seemed like a nice idea, said Mrs. Betts, but what, exactly, would one write inside? So sorry that your marriage ended. Hope you can find a man who'll put up with your crazy daughter? No.

So we delivered baked goods to our neighbor, told her that our husbands would be happy to help with her yard. After the first week, she quit answering the door, though we could tell that she was home. We could hear her in there, watching movies, reading books with Isabella. Sometimes we heard raised voices and, one time, Mrs. Jepsen thought she heard the sound of Mrs. Morrow crying, although it might have been the television, it was hard to say.

11. Orange rake.

Come May, her lawn filled in with rhizomed species

such as we had never seen in our community: the grass surrendering to clover, purslane and wild violets, wherever these could find a ray of sun between the dandelions.

On Mother's Day, long after we had wearied, all, of leaving baked treats on her porch to feed the foxes, raccoons, who knew what other creatures of the night, long after we had given up on tucking flyers for lawn and garden services under her door, we served our neighbor with a fine. Five hundred dollars, for ignoring our repeated pleas to tend her property. Mrs. Taylor worried that the timing was insensitive, but we weren't trying to be cruel. We were only trying to protect her real estate investment.

Later, that same afternoon, she mowed the lawn, for just the second time since her husband had left. The weeds remained. We'd tried so hard. We'd tried to show her she was not alone, but she didn't want our help or our advice and it was this which, like the thorns of that giant thistle growing through her sidewalk, pierced our hearts.

12. ORANGE FISH.

July, and all her dandelions went to seed. The pale fluff swirled around our driveways, marred the surfaces of koi ponds. It clogged the nose of Mrs. Jepson's miniature Schnauzer, made him sneeze. In summertime, we do a lot of entertaining and our guests, that year, were curious about the neo-Tudor with the unkempt lawn. We told them that the owner was away, and this was true— the house sat empty for much of that month. Mrs. Betts had heard that Mrs. Morrow had gone off to visit relatives, but Mrs. Taylor was quite sure our neighbor had been hospitalized—though no one knew why.

We never found out where she'd gone. When she returned, we served her with another fine. She hadn't paid a penny on the first one, so this one was triple the amount and came with an official notice, on association letterhead, reminding her about our three strikes clause. We all felt terrible that it had come to this. We'd tried to reason with her. We had gone, together, to her door: we'd begged her to do take action on those dandelions. She told us she'd stopped using herbicides, and she thought we should stop, as well. She told us that lawn chemicals had all been found to alter brain development in children. After Mrs. Morrow shut the door, our Mrs. Troy said, "Well. It seems a little late for her to worry about that."

13. ORANGE FLOWER.

After the second fine, she mowed her lawn. And the next day, she was in her yard with Isabella, hacking at the ground beneath her shrubs. We watched, peeking between the slats of our Venetian blinds, as, one by one, she dug up all her barberries, her dogwoods, her spireas. Isabella had a set of child-sized tools—a trowel and a spade—but naturally, she was no help at all. She'd scrape a little dirt into a pile, then wander off to spin in circles with her arms extended until we felt nauseous, just from watching her.

At first, we thought our neighbor planned to separate the roots of her perennials before replanting them. It's a good thing to do, as fall approaches. We were proud. We all assumed that our official warning had, at long last, brought her to her senses. We thought that there would be no need for more unpleasantness—or legal action. But that evening, to our horror, she hauled all her shrubs out to the curb and left them there—roots splayed in the direction of the setting sun, a trail of dirt and trampled petals in their wake.

14. ORANGE LEAF.

We grieved for them. The barberries, we mean. Like most of our perennials, they had been special ordered from an Amish nursery, back East.

The next morning, as we steeled ourselves to meet with our association lawyer, she pulled into her driveway with a carload full of flowers. It was August—all the greenhouses were closing out their stock—and here came our neighbor with her daughter and eight flats of bedding plants: tall, droopy-looking things, much past their prime. She must have bought them off a clearance rack somewhere.

They spent the next few hours digging, planting. They filled up the borders, first, with dwarf chrysanthemums. Mrs. Morrow broke the tangled, root-bound flowers from their boxes before handing them to Isabella, who was wearing new fluorescent gloves, with tags, the same hue as those vests that hunters wear. She helped her daughter mound the soil around each plant, after she placed it in the ground. We'd never seen the child stay focused for so long.

Our Neighborhood Association Handbook, Chapter VI: "No changes to existing lawn garden plans shall be initiated without the prior approval of the landscaping committee." Not that we were entirely opposed to those chrysanthemums. Mrs. Jepson said they looked quite festive, with their russet blooms—she thought they were appropriate for fall. But we were undivided in our loathing of the tiger-lilies, which they planted underneath the window, where the barberries had been. The giant flowers were all wrong for that location and besides, as Mrs. Maxwell pointed out, it was the time of year for bulbs, not bedding plants. We were confused and mystified, until we saw what they'd been saving for the corner bed. Two boxes full of marigolds. Well, then we knew.

15. ORANGE ROOT.

The growing season has been very long, this year. We're still awaiting the first killing frost, and meanwhile, we must cope with questions from our visitors. Mrs. Maxwell's houseguest wants to know about the neo-Tudor on the cul-de-sac, about the child in the bright, hooded tracksuit who is watering the flowers, there. The guest laughs, watching as the girl bends, lock-kneed, to sniff every bloom before she sprinkles it, and then the guest points at the woman, kneeling down among the rows of seedlings, by the porch. "What kind of plants are those?"

the guest asks. "Carrots?"

Instead of answering, we talk about the covenants. We tell the visitor about the three-strikes clause, though we can tell that she's not listening at all. She's watching as the child empties her watering can, then flings it skyward and starts spinning, faster, faster, like an orange tornado, arms out, eyes closed, smiling.

Me? I watch Isabella, too, remembering all that I once had, and was—thinking of everything we've lost. I turn away. We've learned to let things go.

Canoe

CHET IS OUTSIDE, HAULING trash-bags to the dumpster, when the car with the canoe pulls up to the first pump. It's the end of April, cold and sunny—the store hasn't had a customer all morning. Taking the trash out is supposed to be Mark's job, but Chet doesn't mind. He likes the fresh air, never tires of these surroundings: snow-capped peaks and ponderosa pines, the nearby murmur of the river. On days like this, Chet thinks that Mark is right: as shit jobs go, this one is not half-bad.

The driver, tall and ruddy-faced, fair-haired, gets out and waves at Chet. Chet waves back, trying to read the license plates. Not local, that's for sure. Nobody from around here would be caught dead in a car with such bald tires. But this guy doesn't look much like the usual out-of-stater, either. In tourist season, Chet sees kayaks nestled atop custom roof-racks, big trailers laden down with boats that probably cost three times as much as Chet makes in a year. He doesn't see too many wood canoes, tied to the top of station wagons with old rope. Especially not this early in the spring, when there are ice chunks in the Middle Fork, in certain spots.

The tall man's standing, staring at the pump. Another day, Chet might just let him stand there, flummoxed, until he read the sign taped to the handle or else got back in his car and drove away, but Chet is feeling generous this morning. His girlfriend, Sandy, has just had her second ultrasound—the doctor says that it's boy, ten fingers and ten toes. So Chet's happy and relieved and anyway, he likes this customer. Most of them ignore Chet altogether, or they stare right through him, searching for something a bit more photogenic, like a four-point buck—a chipmunk, even. This guy waved. Chet slides the latch shut on the bear-proof dumpster and walks over, wiping his hands off on his jeans. "Our pumps here don't take credit cards," he says. "You have to pay inside."

As the man heads towards the store, Chet moves a little closer to the car so he can read the plate (Land of Lincoln—Illinois) and the adjacent sticker (Love your mother earth). He and Mark will laugh about that sticker, later on. Chet sees that the canoe, atop the car, is made of several different kinds of wood. It's not like any boat he's ever seen—it might be some kind of antique, he thinks. Then the passenger side door swings open and a woman gets out, hugging herself and muttering about the cold.

She's tiny, with dark hair cut very short, in a big-city style. She opens the back door and Chet hears the snap of car-seat buckles. "Come on," she says. "Time for a potty break." And two small boys climb out, one light, one dark, just like their parents.

The dark-haired one is older, five or six, maybe. He skirts behind the car, in front of Chet, gives him a somber look. Over the next few days, the journalists will have a lot to say about this boy and how he never seems to smile in photographs. They'll comment on his seriousness as though it must be evidence of something, but Chet thinks that serious is probably how this child was born – it isn't anybody's fault.

The younger boy—who can't be more than three—is wearing a plastic Viking hat, with horns. He takes off running towards the store, holding his arms out sideways, making airplane sounds. Chet watches until the woman and the boys all disappear into the store, then he moves closer to the car. He runs his fingertips along the curving side of the canoe, feeling the silken smoothness of the wood, and wonders which of the two boys his own son will resemble most: will he be quiet or exuberant? Chet makes a fist and raps the boat, once, then again. The sound that answers him is deep and rich, reverberating in the mountain air.

Chet has been working at the store three years. He started when he was in high school and went full-time after graduation. There aren't a lot of jobs to choose from, in these parts. Besides the store, there's just the school and post office and Fuzzy's Bar—which is nothing but a double-wide, and only open half the year. From their graduating class of seven, Chet and his girlfriend are the only ones remaining. One of their old friends moved away to college, another one is selling carpet in Missoula, two joined the Marines, and one's in prison, serving five to ten.

If he weren't going to be a father, soon, what Chet would like to do is go up to Alaska, work the big oil rigs. Not just because it pays well (though he wouldn't mind making a little money, for a change) but because it's dangerous. Chet likes movies about stranded mountain climbers, trapped miners, airplane crash survivors. His social studies teacher once loaned him a book about the Shackleton expedition and he read the whole thing, front to back. But Alaska's not an option anymore, and working at the store is pretty much okay, as shit jobs go. Especially since Mark got hired, full-time.

Before the store, Mark worked at a casino up in Whitefish, but the town was full of assholes, so he left. Mark's funny, for an old guy. Mark's first day, he said, "Hey, Kid, I'll bet you ten bucks I can stand inside the meat locker for fifteen minutes." He did it, too. He sealed himself inside the small refrigerated shed behind the store, a shed their boss built for his other business: processing wild game. When he came out, his lips were almost blue and he had icy sparkles in his hair and eyebrows, like the ghost of Shackleton. "Pay up, d-d-douche-bag," he said, through chattering teeth. Yes, Mark's a blast.

Inside the store, Chet finds Mark leaning on the counter, flipping through a *Rolling Stone*. The tall man's looking at the fishing tackle while his wife is in the bathroom, with their boys. Chet hears the children's voices through the door. The man from Illinois holds up a thin spoon lure for Mark to see. "Hey, how about this one? This one any good?"

"Sure," Mark says, sounding bored. "Like I told you, anything we sell is gonna work, so long as you remember that you're smarter than the fish." Chet wonders if he's being funny. Hard to tell. They both mess with the customers, for kicks; when things get slow, they have fun with tourists—like the time they marked that German couple's map to help them find a colony of jackalopes ("Be sure to go at dusk. They're active then")—but when it comes to fishing, Mark has strange ideas. Chet often invites Mark to go down to the fishing access with him, after work, and cast some flies, but Mark always has some excuse. Chet wonders, sometimes, if his friend is scared of water.

Chet feels bad for the tourist; the lure he's picked out is the wrong one for the fast spring current. It won't sink deep or fast enough to reach the trout, made sluggish by the icy temperatures, this time of year. Chet walks over to the tackle section, finds a box of mid-weight spoons. "Try these."

"Hey, thanks," the man says. "Are these what you use?"

"No. I use flies, mostly. But these lures should do the trick."

Chet sees that Mark is scowling at his magazine, and Chet's face and neck get hot. He walks back past the coolers full of bait and cold drinks, past the cardboard cutout of the woman in the hula skirt, holding a beer, past racks of dream-catchers, made in Taiwan, and hand-tooled leather cell-phone holsters. Chet picks up a holster, wipes the dust off on his sleeve, and puts it back. He should have kept his mouth shut, he knows that.

"Last night we camped near the Missouri river," says the tourist. "What a spot. Looks like it hasn't changed since Lewis and Clark. Woke this morning to a whole field of snow geese, taking off. All around us, it was this white ocean of wings, beating." And he flaps his arms, slow-motion—an absurd thing for a man his size to do. Chet hopes Mark isn't watching this. He's grateful when the man stops flapping and extends his hand. "I'm Brian."

"Chet."

They shake, and Brian says, "We've been on the road almost a week. The boys have never been out west before. Tess wanted to fly but I said no, you get to see things on a road-trip, you know what I mean? I want my kids to remember this forever. You don't get to see stuff, on an airplane."

Chet nods. He's never ridden on a plane. Mark has, plenty of times. Mark even flew up to Alaska, once, though he's kind of vague about the details, when Chet asks.

Brian crouches on his heels and lifts a basket full of caddis flies from a low shelf. Chet wants to tell him it's too early for that hatch, but he's determined not to interfere again.

Chet's parents own a taxidermy shop, where they do trophy mounts: moose, elk and bighorn sheep, along with a few mountain lions, bears and fish. From time to time, their clients bring in poached game, assured that there will be no questions asked. Work hard and mind your own damn business—that's the family motto, a philosophy that's served them well enough, so far.

Since taxidermy doesn't pay the bills, Chet's father also drives a propane truck, five days a week. His mom sells handmade earrings on the internet and cleans vacation cabins. "Cabin" is the wrong word for those log monstrosities, four times the size of any ordinary home, all owned by out-of-staters and all vacant ten months of the year. Chet's mother keeps a pair of sheepskin slippers in her glove compartment, since her clients don't want her scuffing up their hardwood floors with outdoor shoes.

Someday, Chet hopes to have a cabin of his own. Just a little place where he can take his boy and Sandy on the weekends, nothing fancy. Chet's parents never took him anywhere, when he was young. They were too busy working, for one thing, and his dad said: "What's the point? We already live in poor-man's paradise." Chet's mom has never been to Glacier Park, although it's only a half-hour away. She says, "You've seen one tourist, seen them all."

Chet hears the water running in the bathroom. Then the door flies open and the younger boy comes running out, with his mom and brother trailing, at a slower pace. Mark looks Tess up and down as she goes past the checkout stand, and Chet is pretty sure he'll have some things to say about her, later. Mark's never said a single impolite thing about Sandy, though—he's good that way. He has his flaws, but he's a loyal friend. One time, a customer in an expensive-looking ski suit started tearing into Chet about the bathroom, said he hadn't cleaned it thoroughly enough. This was back when Mark first started, and he interrupted: "Lady, where do you think this is—Beverly Hills? If you're too delicate to do your business there, we got a forest right outside the door. Just pick a tree." And when the woman stormed out, furious, he winked at Chet. "You can't let out-of-staters treat you that way, kid. Don't let them think they're better than you, just because they're rich." That was when Mark first started. After that, Chet didn't care about Mark's overly long smoke-breaks, or the way his eyes are often red and out-of-focus.

The three-year-old runs over to the cardboard cutout of the woman with the beer, starts pulling on its hula skirt, making the whole thing sway. "Cole, knock it off," says Tess. "That's not a toy." She looks much older, under the fluorescent lights. She looks tired. Brian turns around, holding a pair of child-sized, plastic fishing poles. "Hey, honey, look at these!"

"We don't need those," she says. "We have some fishing poles already, in the car."

"But the boys would love these. They have racecars on the handle."

"Then why'd we bring the others all this way? Why bring them fifteen hundred miles if you're just going to buy some new ones, on a whim?"

"They're not expensive. See?" Brian tilts the poles to show the price tags but his wife won't look and Chet can tell that Brian's not going to win this argument. Chet wonders if this is how he and Sandy will behave, once they are married. Already, they are fighting about money. Sandy doesn't want to go on living in the basement of his parents' house. Neither does Chet, but what choice do they have? Each morning, after Chet opens the store, he scans the classifieds, looking for someplace cheap to live—a rented trailer, maybe, near some forest service land, a place with lots of room for a young boy to run, but there is nothing. Sandy works at the fish hatchery. She likes her job, but barely makes enough to make up for the gas it takes to get there—forty miles, round trip. And anyway, she'll have to quit before too long.

Now Cole, the little boy, is tugging on Brian's arm. "Please, Daddy, please. I want that racecar pole." His older brother sidles over to the candy rack, inspects a carton full of Tootsie Rolls.

"They're not expensive," Brian repeats.

"That's not the point."

"Can I have a candy?" asks the older boy. Nobody answers him.

Brian hangs the fishing poles back on the rack and Cole bursts into noisy tears. Tess scoops him up. "You're tired. You guys stayed up too late last night," she says, rubbing his back. She carries him out of the store, his Viking hat askew, and his wails grow louder and then softer, as the door closes behind them. "We were looking at the constellations," says the dark-haired boy, to no one in particular. He scoops a handful of square caramels up in one hand and lets them rain back down into the box.

Chet fumbles in his pocket, looking for loose change. He wants to give the boy a dime to buy a candy, but he'll have to do it quick, so Mark won't see. Mark's ringing up Brian's purchase at the moment: two spoon lures, a wooly bugger and some caddis flies. "And give me thirty bucks in gas," says Brian, "and these." He turns and grabs the child-sized fishing poles down off the wall.

"Good man," says Mark. "You can't let them tell you what to do."

Brian squints at him. "You're married?"

"No."

Chet finds a dime and hisses, underneath his breath, trying to get the dark-haired boy's attention. "Can I ask you something?" Brian is saying to Mark. "My guide-book shows a river access close to here."

Mark nods. "Just past the bridge."

"What is it, four or five miles to the next take-out?"

"Yessir. Some real good fishing on that stretch."

"And it's safe?" says Brian. "This time of year? It didn't look like there were any hazards, on the map."

"Oh, hell," says Mark. "Round here, we float it all year round." Chet glanced through the window at the wood canoe, atop the car, then looks back at his friend. Mark can't be serious. No one they know would ever go canoeing now. Not when the rivers are so high and cold. And then, out of the corner of his eye, Chet sees the dark-haired boy slip a caramel into his jacket pocket.

Stop, thief. Chet wants to laugh, watching the boy stand motionless, like that. Chet remembers being his age, he remembers stealing things. The poor kid's heart is probably pounding now. He probably thinks the local sheriff's going to show up with a posse and a rope to hang him high. Well, he doesn't need to worry. Chet's no snitch.

"Hey, thanks," says Brian to Mark. "It's good to talk to someone local, get the scoop. You never know if you can trust these maps, know what I mean? Jasper, come on. It's time to go."

Brian leaves, trailed by his thieving son, and Mark goes back to looking at his magazine. Chet takes the inventory binder and starts ticking through the cigarette list, until he can't stand the silence anymore. "That one boy, Jasper, he just stole a candy," Chet says. "Right in front of me."

Mark shrugs. Outside, Brian is putting gas into the car, his free hand resting on the side of the canoe. The others are already in the car. Chet sees Cole's profile, in his Viking hat; he sees Tess in the passenger seat, smiling. She must not know about the fishing poles, yet. Then Chet thinks of something that has not occurred to him, till now.

"Hey Mark, you don't suppose they're gonna take those little boys out on the river?"

Mark turns another page of *Rolling Stone*. "Look, kid, it's really not my problem what these dipshits do."

Chet drops his pencil and it rolls beneath the beverage cooler, out of sight. For years to come, he will recall that pencil at odd times. When he's brushing his teeth, tucking his young son into bed, he'll hear it, rolling over the linoleum, or picture it shrouded in dust beneath the cooler and then—no matter how hard he resists—he will think about Tess, waiting on the bank, shading her eyes to look upstream, checking her watch, again, wondering where they are.

And the next thing he'll remember is how long he stood there, staring out the window at the car. It took at least two minutes for Brian to finish filling up the tank, another thirty seconds to drive down the frontage road, and even then—after the car was on the highway—it was not too late. Chet could have followed them in his own car; he knew where they were going. At the very least, he could have called someone—the sheriff, maybe, Fish and Game. And though he'll try for years to tell himself the accident was not his fault, that it happened because of Mark or Brian or Tess—deep down, he'll always know where blame resides.

A SUNDAY MORNING, TEN years later, Chet is at the kitchen table with his daughter. They're working on her science fair project, building a display case for the various types of owl pellets she has dissected. With his X-Acto knife, Chet makes an inch-long notch on each side of a square of balsawood and hands the square to Hannah Rose, his only child. It turns out ultrasounds are sometimes wrong.

In the small, adjoining living room, the television's on. No one is watching. Grunt, the dog, is sleeping underneath the burl wood coffee table. On the corner bookshelf is a clock that once belonged to Sandy's great, great aunt, and under this is Sandy's own collection of glass horses. Also a large stuffed-and-mounted weasel that Chet's parents gave them for a wedding present.

Hannah tilts her square of wood and dots some beads of glue along one edge. She's telling Chet about some new girl in her class. "Yeah, Caitlyn thinks she's so cool, just because she went to Disneyland for Christmas."

"Uh-huh," says Chet, only half-listening. He's been helping Hannah with this project for an hour. He stands to stretch, looks through the sliding glass door at the deck he built behind their manufactured home.

"It's true," says his daughter. "Apparently her grandma lives down there. In California."

Through the glass door, Chet can see a herd of deer, walking single-file up the hill, sinking chest-deep in the snow with every step. The hillside is a tangled mesh of tracks—deer, rabbit, fox, raccoon. And Chet's and Hannah's bootprints, marking where they pulled their sleds up, earlier this morning, to slide down the steep bowl on the other side.

"So anyway," Hannah is saying, "Then Caitlyn goes, 'My grandma has a swimming pool in her backyard.' And we're like, 'Hello, we don't care, okay?'"

"Uh-huh." He walks across the kitchen, pours another mug of coffee, puts it in the microwave. While he waits for it to heat, he contemplates the pictures on the fridge. There's Hannah playing on her swingset, Hannah holding up a fish she caught in Glacier Park, Hannah playing the recorder, Hannah swimming in the reservoir below the dam, her red hair fanned out on the surface of the water (people are always telling Chet it's a good thing the girl resembles Sandy, and not him). Here's a crayon drawing Hannah brought home in first grade: herself in a pink dress, with wings. The paper's fading now, and curling at the edges, but Chet doesn't want to take it down. Each time he sees it, he thinks how strange it is that he once thought he would prefer a son.

The bedroom door opens and Sandy comes out in her bathrobe, mug in hand. She goes over to the coffee maker, pours herself the dregs. "So guess who died?"

"Who?" Hannah says.

Chet frowns. "Why aren't you studying?"

"I am," says Sandy, tightening her ponytail. Sandy's been taking online classes in biology. The hatchery would probably pay for Chet to take some classes, too, now that he works there full-time, with his wife. One day, he might just do that, when he's not so occupied with other things, like trying to build an extra room onto their manufactured home, so they'll have space for a piano. Right now, his daughter has to practice on an electronic keyboard, which is not the same.

"I'm studying," says Sandy. "I just saw this story someone posted."

"Surfing the net?" says Chet. "I thought you had a test."

"I do. Remember Lyndon Mackie? Heart attack."

Chet sets his mug down on the counter, hard, splashing hot coffee on his hand.

"Yeah, Mackie. You know him. The game warden who pulled that kid out of the river. You remember?"

Chet nods. He remembers. Every day.

"Yeah, had a heart attack and died. Apparently, the family of that boy is going to fly out for the funeral. All the way from Ohio, or wherever."

"Illinois," says Chet.

"Yeah. Anyway, I think it's nice they're flying out. I bet some people around here will show up at the funeral, just to see what they look like in real life. I'd be curious to see them. Wouldn't you?"

"See who?" says Hannah, making pencil markings on another piece of wood. "What family?"

Chet doesn't speak. His wife is not aware that he met Tess and Brian and their two kids in person, in the store. He's never told a soul about that day. After the accident, he wanted to tell her, or someone, just to get it off his chest, but Chet was too afraid. He thought if Sandy knew what happened, she would never speak to him again.

"I admire them for coming back," says Sandy. "Must be really hard. Remember all those letters people wrote?"

"What letters?" Hannah says.

"Tell you later," Chet says. And someday, he will. Someday he'll tell his daughter everything. He'll even tell her about how angry people were when the papers ran that picture, the next day. A photo Tess had taken, right before the launch: her husband and her two sons at the river's edge, all wearing lifejackets, all holding paddles with the blades up, towards the sunny sky. Brian and Cole are grinning; Jasper's not. The older boy's afraid—that's what one person wrote, some stranger who had never met the boy. You can see it in his eyes. The poor kid's terrified. And there were lots of other letters to the editor, many of them saying that Brian and Tess should be locked up for negligence. One woman, writing from someplace in West Virginia, said Tess was a disgrace to motherhood.

"I still don't understand why anyone would take a risk like that." Sandy sniffs a gallon jug of milk that Chet's left open, on the counter. "I mean, they looked like normal people, on T.V. You done with this?"

Chet puts the milk back in the fridge, remembering Lyndon Mackie on the television news, that melancholy face. You grow up here, you see a lot of tourists doing stupid things, but this.…And Chet remembers how the warden's voice cracked as he told about the plastic Viking hat that he found floating in the reeds, a quarter mile upstream from where he found the little boy, face-down in shallow water, his lifejacket snagged in between two rocks. Mackie had pulled the boy ashore and started CPR. He'd kept the chest compressions going right until the paramedics got there, twenty minutes later, though he understood that it was hopeless. Cole was gone. He had no pulse at all.

"Are you all right?" asks Sandy. "You look terrible."

"Headache." Chet says, and rubs the space between his eyes. How would it be if he saw Tess and Brian now, he wonders? Would they recognize him, after all this time? What would they say? If Chet could talk to them, he'd tell them that he never went back to his job, after that day—he couldn't stand to see Mark's face again. And would it make a difference if he told them that he knew the real reason their older son looked worried, in that photograph? He wasn't psychic—he just had a stolen candy in his pocket, that was all.

Jasper the thief. Chet wonders how he looks now, in

his teens. And Cole, the little one. He must be at least twelve years old by now.

Because he lived—that was the part nobody could believe. The reason that the story made the national news and Lyndon Mackie got to make appearances on morning talk-shows.

ALMOST TWO HOURS WITHOUT vital signs—two hours, during which time the child is helicoptered to one hospital, and then another, with an oxygen mask covering his face (the paramedics see no point to this—the boy is clearly gone—but protocol is protocol). Two hours, two hospitals, a tube inserted down the throat to bathe his organs in warm saline, while physicians argue. Three of them say Cole is dead. The fourth, an intern, disagrees. He isn't dead until he's warm and dead. And meanwhile, while the doctors argue, the boy's blood is being sucked out of his veins and run through a dialysis machine to heat it up, then pumped back into his limp arm, on towards his blue, unbeating heart. And the noisy machine goes on suctioning and pumping while Brian and Tess are in the next room, saying nothing to each other—he is sitting with his face between his knees and she is pacing back and forth along the far wall, until the chaplain comes into the room and tries to touch her shoulder and she screams and claps her hands over her ears and screams and screams some more. And the second-oldest doctor tells the intern, in a soft voice: time to face the facts, kid. We did everything we could. In the midst of all this, at the precise moment when the temperature reading on the monitor blips up to ninety-six degrees, the boy opens his eyes.

Alive, and—this is stranger still—unchanged. No damage to his brain, his heart, no frostbite, even. No lasting consequences, save a tendency towards nightmares where he wakes up swimming, struggling to breathe.

"IF YOUR HEAD HURTS, take some Tylenol," says Sandy. And she goes back in the bedroom, shuts the door.

"Dad," Hannah says. "Can you cut this for me, now? I drew a line."

Chet picks up his X-Acto knife and tests the sharpness of the blade against his thumb. After the accident, the television networks brought on experts to explain a thing called the Mammalian Dive Reflex: a subject Chet has spent a lot of time researching on his own. He spent too many hours, on the internet, reading about vestigial survival mechanisms and the sometimes unpredictable effects of rapid-onset hypothermia in children, trying to understand how human brains retain abilities developed back when mammals all had fins instead of legs. Eventually, he had to give it up. There are some things, Chet has decided, that cannot be explained by science alone. Like his own daughter's entrance to the world, Cole's resurrection was an act of grace.

"IS THIS THE LAST one?" Chet asks, cutting wood.

"Yes. Next I have to glue the felt inside. How come you won't tell me about those people from Ohio?"

"Illinois," says Chet. "It's a long story. Anyway, you never finished telling me about this new kid. What's her name?"

"Caitlyn."

"Oh, right. Caitlyn. From Great Falls."

"No, Dad, she's from Billings. Weren't you listening? She came from Billings and she's always bragging. Like, my old school had an auditorium and this one doesn't even have a gym. My old school had a library. Big deal."

Chet puts his knife down, strokes his stubbled chin. "You should invite her over. We could take her snow-mobiling, maybe."

"What? Are you kidding? She's a total snob."

"She's probably lonely. You should find out what she's doing tomorrow, after school."

Hannah is staring at him, open-mouthed, one eye-brow raised. It's an expression Chet has grown accustomed to, of late. Gone are the days when his small daughter thought he was the smartest man alive. He doesn't mind. This is the price he has to pay.

"Invite her," Chet says. "Please." He wants so many things for Hannah Rose. He wants his child to know about the threads—invisible, like fishing line—that connect her to the world and every person in it.

ACKNOWLEDGMENTS

The author is grateful to the following journals, where several of the stories in this collection first appeared:

"Schooling" in *New Letters*; "Leah, Lamb" in *The Hudson Review*; "Jester" in *Crazyhorse*; "Monsters of the Deep" in *Arts & Letters*; "14 Tips for Selling Real Estate" in *Quarterly West*; "Covenants" in *Indiana Review*; "Fun with Color" in The Tampa Review; "Canoe" in *Crab Orchard Review*; and "Vaquero" in *Prairie Schooner*.

ABOUT THE AUTHOR

Dana Fitz Gale has won numerous awards for her fiction, which has recently appeared in *The Hudson Review, Crazyhorse, Prairie Schooner, Indiana Review, Quarterly West, New Letters, Mid-American Review, Arts & Letters, Crab Orchard Review, New South, Tampa Review*, and elsewhere. She lives on a small farm in Montana with her husband, two sons, and assorted dogs, cats, and horses. To learn more, visit danafitzgale.com.